This book is dedicated
to my loved ones,
both near and far,
whom I would never have known
were it not for the
system of adoption.

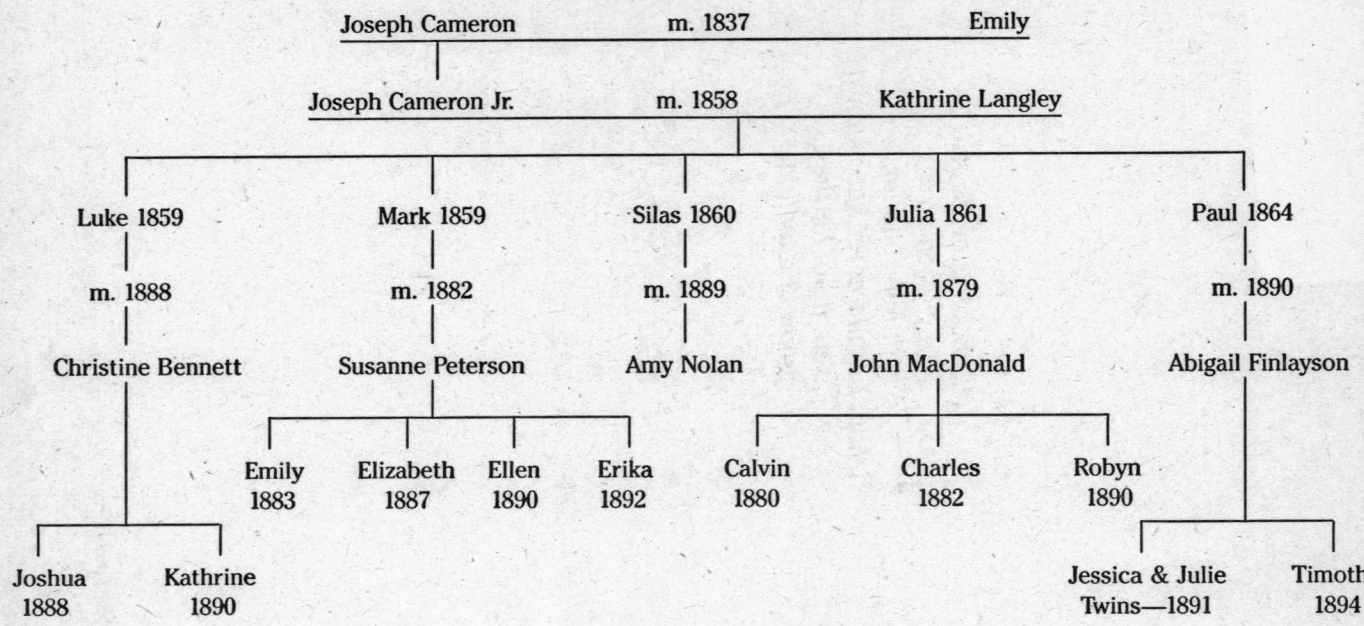

CAMERON FAMILY TREE — 1894

Joseph Cameron   m. 1837   Emily

Joseph Cameron Jr.   m. 1858   Kathrine Langley

Luke 1859	Mark 1859	Silas 1860	Julia 1861	Paul 1864
m. 1888	m. 1882	m. 1889	m. 1879	m. 1890
Christine Bennett	Susanne Peterson	Amy Nolan	John MacDonald	Abigail Finlayson

Emily 1883   Elizabeth 1887   Ellen 1890   Erika 1892

Calvin 1880   Charles 1882   Robyn 1890

Joshua 1888   Kathrine 1890

Jessica & Julie Twins—1891   Timothy 1894

A Gathering of Memories

LORI WICK

HARVEST HOUSE PUBLISHERS
Eugene, Oregon 97402

All Scripture quotations in this book are taken from the King James Version of the Bible.

Except for certain well-established place names, all names of persons and places mentioned in this novel are fictional.

Music and lyrics for "Song for the Other Mary" by Timothy Barsness and Lori Wick. Used by permission.

Cover by Terry Dugan Design, Minneapolis, Minnesota

A Place Called Home Series
A Place Called Home
A Song for Silas
The Long Road Home
A Gathering of Memories

A GATHERING OF MEMORIES

Copyright © 1991 by Harvest House Publishers
Eugene, Oregon 97402

Library of Congress Cataloging-in-Publication Data
Wick, Lori.
    A gathering of memories / Lori Wick
      Sequel to: The long road home.
    ISBN 1-56507-591-9
    I. Title. II. Series.
  PS3573.I237G37 1991
  813'.54—dc20   91-13604
                                     CIP

Printed in the United States of America.

01 02 03 04 05 / BC / 15 14 13 12 11

1

"Sweetheart. Are you nearly ready? We're going to be late for church." Silas spoke to his wife as he entered their bedroom.

Amy, hairpins in her mouth, did not answer. Silas watched her face in the mirror for a moment before going on in a gentle voice. "It would be better for both of us if you tell me before church what you're upset about."

Amy made a slight pause in her preparations but then rushed on, hairpins nearly flying, without answering.

Minutes later they were in the buggy, headed for church. "I thought you said we were going to be late." This time it was Silas who did not respond.

"Silas, why are you driving so slowly?"

Silas answered, his voice a caress. "I'm driving slow hoping that my wife will tell me what is bothering her before we get to the church."

He heard her sigh deeply and waited, hoping she would at last confide in him.

"I'm not pregnant." She admitted quietly.

Silas brought the team to a complete halt in the middle of the road and turned on the seat to look at her, a look she wouldn't return. He watched her profile for a moment, having known that this month was going to be worse because they'd taken care of their nephew and niece, Joshua and Kate, two weeks ago, while Luke and Christine took a short trip.

"You must be sick to death of me telling you I'm not pregnant," Amy spoke before Silas could say anything. Quietly she added, "Probably sick to death of me, too."

He leaned forward and put his face so close to her own she had no choice but to look at him. "You know better, Amy. There is nothing that can change my love for you."

Appearing totally unconvinced, she was shocked with Silas' next words. "Did you ever think that I might be the reason that we've been married over five years and you've never been pregnant?"

"What?"

"I'm serious. Did you ever think that there might be something in me, in my body, and the way I'm put together that's keeping us from having children?"

"No, that's ridiculous."

"Why is it ridiculous?"

"I don't know. I've just never heard of such a thing."

"And that makes it ridiculous?" They sat in silence for a time, both praying.

"Amy."

"Silas." They spoke in unison and then shared a small laugh. "You go first," Silas said.

"I was praying just now and thinking about what you said, and I don't think it really matters—the whys and who's, that is. It might be that there is something in one or both of us that keeps us from conceiving. Either way, it's God's way, and I'm going to have to accept that. If it were God's will that I be pregnant, I would be.

"I'm afraid I don't remember that as often as I need to, and I'm sorry if I made you feel inadequate in any way. If God has children for us, He will give them to us in His time."

Silas pulled her into his arms and held her close.

"I love you, Si."

"I love you, too, and I was thinking the exact same thoughts. I've always believed that you're my gift from God, and nothing on this earth is more important than you are."

They kissed then. Silas' embrace tightened a moment before Amy suddenly pushed from his arms, her hands on his chest to hold him at bay.

"Silas," she reprimanded him, "I just put those pins in my hair, and we are already late for church."

He didn't take his eyes from her as she smoothed her

hair, and his look told her they would finish this conversation later. Amy smiled with loving confidence as he urged the team toward town.

They were indeed very late for church. Slipping soundlessly into a rear pew, they listened to a sermon that was well underway.

Pastor Nolan's text was on love for each other and Amy thought how special it was to be in her Uncle Chad's church. He was a man who loved God with all of his heart and whose sermons never failed to encourage her even when she was faced with her sin.

They realized just how late they were, when ten minutes after they sat down, Pastor Nolan brought the sermon to a close with serious words.

"I have a special prayer request to ask of you this morning. I was called out last night to the Jackson home. Most of you know of the Jacksons; they live on the edge of town. Mrs. Jackson died yesterday, and Mr. Jackson has not been located. There are five children ranging from 5 to 18 years old and I'm worried about them. The funeral for Mrs. Jackson will be Tuesday morning, and well, please be remembering this family in your prayers."

The congregation stood for the closing hymn and prayer, but Amy heard none of the song. Her uncle had just said "Amen" when Amy spoke.

"Silas, I want those children."

"What did you say?" He bent over her, listening closely as she spoke in almost a whisper.

"I said, I want those children."

Silas stared at her. His mind raced as he remembered everything he'd ever heard about the Jackson children—"a very unruly bunch" was the nicest, he was sure. No, that was not quite right. The two oldest, both girls, were said to be fairly well-behaved. But the three youngest, two boys and another girl, he thought, were as wild as they came. But he somehow knew that even if it were true, it wouldn't matter to her. Another tact was needed here.

'Amy, sweetheart, they have a father."

"But Uncle Chad said he isn't here right now, and until he can be found I want those children to come and live with us."

Silas opened his mouth and then closed it. She stared up at him, entreaty filling her wide blue eyes, making Silas feel helpless.

"Sweetheart," he tried again. "You probably haven't heard about this family. I don't really know them myself, but you see they have a reputation for being unmanageable." Silas put it as delicately as possible, but exactly as he expected, a stubborn look crossed his wife's face.

"They're children, Silas, one only five years old. And I don't care if they have no manners whatsoever. They need someone to take care of them, and we have no reason that I can think of *not* to open our home to those children."

Again Silas stared at her. "We'll talk to your uncle," Silas spoke quietly. Amy's answer was equally quiet, her eyes shining with gratitude. "Thank you, Silas."

2

Silas and Amy were already planning to have lunch with Chad and April Nolan so Silas did not have long to wait to talk with Amy's uncle. April Nolan was a wonderful cook and the meal of roast pork, baked potatoes, turnip greens, fresh bread, and coffee was just beginning when Silas brought up the subject.

His wife's uncle listened in silence as the entire story came out. When Silas was done he had a question for Silas alone.

"Every time you spoke, Silas, you said 'Amy wants.' What do you want? It's your home, too. Do you have misgivings you're not voicing?"

"Definitely. You probably wouldn't believe how many."

"Try me." The simple words from Chad were enough to break the dam around Silas' unsure heart.

"First of all, I've heard that the three youngest Jacksons are as wild as they come." Silas held one hand in the air and counted his fingers as he spoke.

"Secondly, the oldest is not that much younger than my wife, and has, I'm sure, a mind of her own. If I recall, Mrs. Jackson never enjoyed good health. I imagine that oldest girl runs everything and probably has for a long, long time. I'm also horrified at the thought that they'll move into our hearts as well as our home. Then to have Mr. Jackson return, take them all away and break Amy's heart, not to mention my own...

"And the thing that has me most bothered is, is it really our business? I mean, we can't just go over there and say 'you're coming with us' and expect them to just cheerfully follow a couple of near-strangers across town!"

"Actually, you can." Pastor Nolan spoke quietly. "That is, with everyone but Mandy, since she's an adult. I spoke with

Rufus last night and he told me, as sheriff, that it's within his legal rights to place the four younger ones in foster care. He was quite upset because he knows no one will take even one of them, let alone four. He said it would probably be easier, if not best all around, to leave them with their sister since she is old enough to take care of them."

Silas let the words sink in and then looked to his wife. She spoke to him in quiet submission. "Si, I do want those children, but *not* if you're against it. Uncle Chad is right. It isn't just my home; it's our home. Until you spoke all I could picture were summer nights in the yard, popping corn over the fire, sending the children off to school, and well, all of those homey things a family does.

"But you're right. The whole thing could be disastrous, and if your answer is no, I understand. It doesn't mean I couldn't go visit and take them something and try to help in that way."

"But you still want them—I mean, your first choice is to have them come live with us?"

"Yes." The word was spoken without hesitation.

Silas looked at his wife for a long time. She would be wonderful for those children, and he knew it. Oh, there would be adjustments, even if their time together was brief, but if Amy touched their lives for only two days it would be with warmth and caring.

"Where is Mr. Jackson?" Silas posed the question to Chad but never took his eyes from Amy.

"He hasn't been here for some time. Rufus planned to start checking around today."

"You haven't said anything, April. What are your thoughts?" The question came from Pastor Nolan to his wife. All eyes swung to the serene woman at the end of the table who answered unselfconsciously and without haste.

"I always look for reasons for things the Lord brings into my world, and this time was no different. But even though I accepted Chad's news last night when he came home, I couldn't think of one good reason for Mrs. Jackson to die.

And I'm not saying now that I'm glad she did. But the fact is she is gone and her children are left here alone; but this! This...possible plan to take those children in, gives me hope for them. Silas and Amy would be wonderful for them, and I can't help but pray that it works out and that all of us—you and I, Chad, Grandma Em, all the Camerons and MacDonalds—each of us, can play a part in their lives that otherwise would have been impossible."

Silas looked at his pastor's wife. Her words made him understand, for the first time, that Amy wasn't the only one involved. His whole family would be drawn in, but mostly him. Since they would live beneath his roof, he would automatically be a part of their lives too, He could either reach out to them in love, or tolerantly abide them in his house just to give Amy her wish.

The decision was made.

"Amy?" Silas spoke. "Is today too soon?"

"No Silas, today is fine. I baked bread yesterday, and all the beds upstairs are freshly made."

Amy reached for her husband's hand, both wondering as she did, what the next few hours would bring.

3

Silas and Chad rode in silence toward the Jackson home. They had been to see the sheriff, and he had been relieved to hear the situation was well in hand. Rufus had said to come for him if any need arose.

As Silas pulled the large wagon to a stop, he knew he'd never been to this home before. He had probably seen it from a distance but not close enough to tell him that the roof was deteriorating so badly. He doubted whether one inch of the interior stayed dry during a storm.

A rusty plow lay against the weathered siding along with a broken pitchfork, a potato basket, and a large tin can. None of these looked as though they'd just been tossed there but rather placed carefully in order.

In fact a quick look around the yard showed that someone had a care as to how it looked. The weeds around the front of the house were high, but the path to the door was well beaten down and not cluttered with things to trip a man. It was swept clean, right down to the hard earth and was lined with a few small stones.

Silas took all of this in as he followed Chad to the front door, a door that opened before them without a knock. The young woman standing across the threshold was very thin, with dark brown hair. She wore a dress that was too big and a look that was far from welcoming.

"Hello, Mandy. I know you didn't expect to see me until Tuesday but I need to talk with you."

"What about?" The question was asked warily, and the oldest Jackson child made no move to invite him in.

Yes, what about? Chad thought to himself, now that they were here facing this young woman and not sitting around his own dining table, it would not be so easy explaining that her brothers and sisters were to be taken out of her care.

He took a breath and plunged in. "I've been in touch with the sheriff, and he informs me that in cases such as yours the children under age usually stay with families in town until the parent can be found."

Amanda Jackson felt as if the floor beneath her had moved, so shocked was she. Leaning against the doorjamb to steady herself, her mind raced. Silas very nearly reached for her, thinking she was going to faint. Gone instantly was the belief this girl would be strong-minded. She didn't appear ready to question Chad's statement at all. In fact, if he didn't believe with all of his heart how good this would be for these children, he would feel she was very much a victim right now.

"Mandy," Chad's voice was gentle. "If you'll let us in I'll explain everything to you."

Wordlessly she swung the door back and led the way to the table. Silas had never seen a home so lacking in warmth in spite of the humid June day. Not until after he'd sat down at the table, in a chair so beat up he was not sure it would hold his weight, did he notice the occupied bed in the corner.

He was still staring at the bed, or rather the four children sitting on it, when he heard Chad speak.

"Mandy, this is Silas Cameron."

"Hello, Mandy," Silas said to the silent girl at the table, who was still looking numb with surprise.

"And over here on the left is Carrie, she's 14. Sitting next to her is Levi who's ten and then Clovis who's nine, and next to Clovis is Rebecca. Rebecca is five." Silas smiled at each one, but only the little one returned his smile or made any move to acknowledge his introduction.

Silas took none of this personally. He realized how, in the space of a few hours, these children's world had been turned upside down. He only hoped Amy would be as practical. She might respond to their indifference with hurt feelings, but then, maybe not. After all, Amy had lost her mother, too.

Chad explained briefly who Silas was and how he and Silas were related. He then explained the plans to have all five of the children come with them, that very day, to the Cameron home to live.

"You mean you want me to come, too?" Mandy's look was both a mixture of fear and relief as she posed the question to the big man across the table.

"Yes," Silas answered simply thinking what an awful thing it was to assume you were unwanted.

"All five of us, at the same house?"

"Yes."

"For how long?"

"As long as you need."

Suddenly Mandy understood. "What would our jobs be?"

Silas stared at her, completely nonplussed. Chad was the first to recover. "Mandy, you are not being put to work. Silas and Amy have a large home and wish you to share it for as long as you need. They have no ulterior motive, believe me."

Mandy's eyes went from one man to the other, gauging their sincerity, and then to her family. Rebecca must have missed what was going on, for her look was only curious, but Carrie and the boys were looking at her, their eyes round with surprise. Mandy came to a swift decision, wondering as she did, what in the world she would do if it was a mistake.

"Alright," she said as she rose from the table. "We'll come if you really mean the offer."

"Great!" Silas said and stood with her. His smile was so genuine that it was a few minutes before Mandy's qualms returned, and by then she had her siblings gathering their things to leave.

The quilts were removed from the beds and the needed possessions loaded inside. When the first quilt was carried out by the boys, with hardly a bulge within, Silas very nearly sent them back with the order to gather *all* of their things. Just in time he realized they had done just that. He turned away, swallowing hard over the sudden lump in his throat.

A few seconds elapsed before Silas realized the boys had remained next to the wagon and were staring up at him in unembarrassed curiosity. He took his first good look at them. Unlike their oldest sister, whose dress was too big, their clothing was too small, even for their too-thin bodies. But somehow it didn't detract from a look of promised sturdiness.

Their hair, in need of cutting, was dark brown like Mandy's and their eyes were a mixture of browns and greens. Hazel, he guessed it would be called. He studied them as closely as they studied him before admitting he'd forgotten which was Levi and which was Clovis.

"I'm Levi."

"I'm Clovis."

The names were spoken solemnly and Silas studied them an instant longer to put the name with the face. It wasn't hard. Levi was a shade taller and, Silas remembered, older. Clovis had an adorable sprinkling of freckles across the bridge of his nose.

"I'm Silas," he spoke to Levi first and held out his hand. There was a moment's hesitation and then with dawning respect the boy let his hand be swallowed by Silas'.

The act was repeated with Clovis who, with his hand still engulfed in Silas', said, "Our pa's not as big as you."

Silas smiled his slow smile and reached out to tousle the overlong hair of the youngest boy. "We best see if your sister needs help."

The boys followed his broad back to the house and watched him duck beneath the low door. Behind him, they exchanged a look of wonder mixed with a little bit of fear.

4

"Mandy, Silas and I talked it over and he'd really like to see you to the house and let you get settled. You'll be well taken care of, I promise you."

"Thank you, Reverend Nolan," Mandy spoke humbly as he stepped down from the wagon in front of the parsonage.

"Most of the kids at church call me Pastor Chad and the pleasure has been all mine, Mandy. You'll like Amy when you meet her, and if you need me, Silas will bring you." He reached out then with a gentle hand and touched each child as he said good-bye. Their smiles were a little strained, but they all waved at him.

"All set?" Silas asked.

"All set." Mandy answered as the wagon pulled away.

Mandy and Carrie's eyes met as the large farmhouse came into view. It was a beautiful home, two stories of white-painted boards and clean glass. A small, covered porch led to the front door and Mandy, realizing how quickly they would be inside, regretted their lack of privacy.

The two girls were very close and Mandy knew Carrie would have been the perfect person with whom to discuss all this, but there just hadn't been time.

It wasn't anything the men had said or done, but Mandy was sure that if she didn't snatch up this offer, even if it wasn't all it seemed to be, it would disappear forever beyond her grasp and she would be sorry for the rest of her life.

When Pastor Nolan had said something about the different families in town, Mandy had felt lightheaded with panic. That they might actually be separated when they needed so desperately to be together was just too painful to take in. Her heart pounding as the wagon came to a stop, Mandy's fear over what was in store for them in this strange house with these unfamiliar people nearly choked her. Only one thought kept her going: *We're all together and that's exactly what Mama would have wanted.*

Silas could have reassured her so easily if he'd known what she was thinking, but Mandy kept her tempestuous thoughts to herself. It would be some time before she really understood why this family was so willing to take them into their sphere.

Mandy's feet had barely touched the ground when she looked up to see the most beautiful woman she'd ever seen coming toward her. Her mind formed the word "Amy" just as the woman reached her and spoke.

"You must be Mandy. I'm Amy, and I'm so glad you're here."

Mandy was speechless for a moment. *Why she's not much older than I am*, she thought, *and she's beautiful.* Mandy's hand went down the skirt of her dress, realizing for the first time that she must look like a scarecrow compared to this vision of warmth and grace in front of her.

"You are Mandy? I mean, I did get your name right?"

"Yes," Mandy recovered quickly. "I'm Amanda Jackson."

"Which do you prefer, Mandy or Amanda?"

"Mandy, please."

"Then Mandy it is. And you must be Carrie."

"Yes, ma'am." Amy smiled and reached out to squeeze the arm of the younger girl. "Will it be a problem, Carrie, for you to share a bedroom with Rebecca?"

There was a moment of silence before Carrie answered quietly, "No, no problem."

Levi, Clovis, and Rebecca were introduced, and the boys found the same question about sharing a room posed to them. Levi answered as his sister had, and Clovis simply stared at Amy in silence.

Silas led the way through the front door directly to the stairway. Mandy and Amy brought up the rear and with every step Mandy wondered where she would sleep. As they all entered a long narrow room, the first at the top of the stairs, Mandy figured that these people were rich and that there must be a servant with whom she would share quarters.

The room was done in peach and cream, with touches of brown and tan. It was easily twice as long as it was wide with a built-in closet at one end. There was no wallpaper but the peach walls were not marked or scratched in any way. It boasted two broad windows that looked out at a cluster of huge oak trees and *two* brass beds, one at each end of the room. The children looked around in open-mouthed awe as Amy spoke.

"This room is for Carrie and Rebecca. You can each have a bed and if you need anything, just ask."

Amy tried not to look at the vulnerable, unbelieving faces of the two younger girls as she moved back out the door. "Levi and Clovis," she said to the boys, "your room is at the end of the hall at the front of the house."

Everyone moved again, even the ones who already had a room assignment, to see the boys' room. It was square and Amy had chosen every imaginable shade of blue, from pastels to navy. The walls were light blue with a large round rug in bolder shades. It had a masculine feel to it, with dark oak furniture and a wide bed the boys would share. The one large window was throwing sun across that bed now, and they stood gaping at the multicolored quilt as though fascinated.

"Be sure and check with me if you need something boys. Mandy, your room is just a few steps back down the hall."

Nothing in Mandy's imagination could have prepared her for the last bedroom they entered. The room was a vision in softest pink and white and utterly the most feminine decor she had ever seen. The curtains covering the two windows were white and ruffly, as was the coverlet on the large bed. The wallpaper was pink-and-white stripe with small sprigs of lavender flowers every few inches.

Mandy was still taking it all in when Silas ushered the

rest of the Jackson family to their own rooms with a suggestion that they use the dressers within and get themselves settled.

Amy was ready to ask if there was anything Mandy needed when her new houseguest turned to her with an unreadable look on her face.

"Who else stays in here?" Her voice and face did nothing to betray her tenseness, but her stance was almost that of one who expected a blow.

"No one. The room is yours."

"What about you, I mean, I didn't notice a fourth bedroom up here."

"We're downstairs, the door near the foot of the stairs. Mandy, is there something wrong, I mean with the room, that you're not comfortable?"

"No, I just wasn't expecting, I mean, a room all to myself is a new experience."

"Well, I hope you enjoy it and please, like I told your sisters and brothers, don't hesitate to ask if you need something. I'll go now and let you get settled."

Amy started for the door but then came back and put her hands on Mandy's arms. "I want you to know how sorry I am about your mother. I won't keep bringing it up because I know how painful it is, but if you ever want to talk, I'm a good listener." Amy drew Mandy into her arms and hugged her before exiting and closing the door behind her.

5

Amy wondered as she descended the stairs if her legs were going to give out under her. She found Silas in the kitchen and walked straight into his arms. He felt her tremble and held her tightly against his chest.

"Did you see their faces?" Amy finally asked.

"Yes." Silas was thankful as he answered that Amy had not seen where they lived.

"I hugged Mandy, and Silas, there is nothing to her. We seem to be the same height but she must be 20 pounds lighter."

"You can begin changing that tonight at our table." He sounded very confident and indeed he was. He had been sure of God's leading, even though everything had moved so swiftly, especially going for the children. The more time he spent with them the more he believed that he and Amy had been given a special job from the Lord. A job that would definitely change the quiet way they lived and could very well break their hearts. But it was what God called them to do at this time and they would do it.

The five objects of Silas and Amy's thoughts were all gathering in Mandy's room. Mandy had sunk down to the floor and leaned against the wall after Amy left. She was lost in her thoughts when the door opened quietly and Rebecca came in. Mandy held out her arms and Rebecca went into her big sister's lap. The boys came next, sitting down in front of her so their legs touched hers through her skirt. Carrie came last and put Mandy's few things on the bed before taking a spot against the wall, her shoulder against Mandy's.

"Did you get your things put away?" The question was directed to Levi.

"Yeah. There's hooks in the closet and we hung stuff in there."

"How about you, Becca?"

"Carrie did it."

"Where's their bedroom?" Carrie asked.

"Downstairs—and *their* names are Silas and Amy."

"Do we call them Silas and Amy?" Levi sounded incredulous.

"I think so. It's the way they've introduced themselves, but maybe we should say Mr. and Mrs. Cameron until we have permission."

"I think Mrs. Cameron is pretty."

"Oh, Carrie, you're so dumb!"

"Yeah, dumb, Carrie."

"Levi and Clovis, you stop that right now! We are guests in this house and you will mind your manners or I promise you a licking you won't soon forget. Do you hear me?"

"Yes." They answered quietly. Mandy rarely scolded them, but when she did she meant it.

"Where do you think Pa is?"

"I don't know, Clovis. This is the longest he's ever been away. The Reverend Nolan, I mean Pastor Chad, said the sheriff is trying to find him."

"Is that why the—you know—isn't 'til Tuesday?"

"Yes, and it's called a funeral." The word seemed to have a quieting effect on all of them, and even though the day was warm they sat without speaking, huddled together, for a long time.

— ✣ —

Amy's first reaction to having these children at their supper table for the first time was to put out an elaborate spread. But she refrained from such an action and stayed with her normal Sunday evening routine of sandwiches with meats and cheeses along with whatever fruit was in season and cookies for dessert.

As she stood over the breadboard with a knife, she said a prayer of thanks that she'd baked bread yesterday, even though it wasn't her usual day. Not that she couldn't skip over to Christine's, whose house was a stone's throw away, and borrow a loaf, but it was just nice to know she could take care of these five charges, whom she felt were on loan from God.

As Amy sliced, her mind dwelt on Mandy's face and the way she prepared herself for disappointment at every turn. The other ones were easy, even Carrie at 14; they were just children. But Mandy was nearer her own age and if the truth be known, she scared Amy to death. She seemed the most vulnerable and the most in need of mothering. But there was no way with Amy being only 22 that Mandy was going to look at her as a mother figure. After all Mandy was 18. That's why it was so important that she do nothing to make Mandy feel young or patronized and that she do everything to show she wanted to be her friend.

She began to pray as she carried the bread platter to the table that God would give her an opportunity to share the loss of her own mother. Of course she'd had her dad, still had him for that matter, so she couldn't completely understand. Maybe Mandy would throw that in her face...

"Oh, Lord," she prayed as she went to call everyone to supper, "it's all too much for me to take in. Please just use me."

— ✛ —

Silas helped Rebecca wash her hands and they were the last to sit at the dining room table. Amy had left the seating arrangement to Silas and after filling a pitcher with cold water, joined them to find all the girls on one side and the boys on the other.

Silas sat at the head of the table with his back to the windows and Amy took the other end near the kitchen door. As soon as Amy was seated her eyes quickly scanned the table to see if anything was wanting before looking to Silas in expectation of the prayer. His prayer was simple and heartfelt as always, and Amy raised her head to smile at him.

But the smile died on her lips as her gaze took in Clovis and Levi and the looks on their young faces. Hungry children. No, not just hungry children—*starving* children.

Her gaze moved slowly to the other side of the table to find their sisters in the same state. All five of them stared at the platters of meat, bread, and cheese as though they'd never eaten. She saw Clovis' tongue run over his lips, and it was almost her undoing.

Her eyes flew to Silas' and his look told her he hadn't missed any of their faces including her own, which had gone very pale and then flushed all in the space of a few seconds.

"Amy," he said almost sternly to rescue them both. "Please fill the glasses as we start the platters around."

"Oh, certainly," she said a bit too gaily and jumped up with her cheeks red and her eyes a little dazed. But the children took no notice. Their eyes were on the food, such bounty as they'd never seen before.

Amy barely made it through the meal. She vacillated between horror at her own stupidity over not realizing how hungry they must have been when they arrived two hours ago, and worrying that they would make themselves sick by overeating. She wanted to assure them that there was plenty of food and that they need not store up, as she watched the boys swallowing almost without chewing, but she kept silent and just asked God to intervene on behalf of these little ones for more than just their physical appetites.

Mandy and Carrie pitched in with the dishes without being asked and cleanup was quick and easy. Silas played the piano and told the younger children a funny story. It was still early when he announced bedtime, but no one complained. Without too much confusion Amy helped settle Rebecca into bed; Silas took care of the boys and all were asleep within 15 minutes of the lamp being blown out.

After Silas' final check on the younger ones, he went to his own room to find his wife lying across the bed trying to muffle her sobs against a pillow. He immediately lay down beside her and put his arm over her without moving her. Believing she needed to cry, he said nothing to coax her out of her tears, only wishing to comfort her with his presence.

She was physically and emotionally spent when the tears stopped and Silas, with gentle hands, helped her with her gown, took the pins from her hair, and put her under the covers.

Amy fell asleep with her head on his shoulder and Silas, a bit drained himself and knowing tomorrow would be just as busy as today, fell quickly asleep. His mind was on the kids meeting all the nieces and nephews and how much his grandmother was going to love these additions to the family.

6

Silas said nothing the next morning but he knew the exact moment Amy awakened. She shifted close to him, seeking the warmth she'd moved from in the night. Knowing he was always awake first, she immediately began to talk.

"Do you think they slept well?"

"Oh, sure." The answer was much too casual.

"How many times were you up, Si?"

"Three."

Amy was chagrined at not having known any of this, so heavy a sleeper was she. "You can't do that every night. You'll be exhausted."

"I'm fine. You know how fast I fall asleep."

That was quite true. Silas always fell asleep quickly but was a light sleeper. Amy, as a rule, took longer to fall asleep, but when she did, a steam train through the room could not disturb her.

"I was so surprised when Mandy called you Mr. Cameron, and then when Carrie used *Mrs.* Cameron, well, I felt like an antique."

Silas' laughter vibrated the bed. "I can't say as I blame them for not being sure. You forget, I'm 10 years older than you. Levi, Clovis, and Becca could easily be my own."

"Well, no matter. They know now that you're Silas and I'm Amy."

"How should we introduce my family?"

"Well, Gram is Grandma Em to everyone. Luke and Christine and the rest can be Uncle Luke or whatever, just like they are to all the nieces and nephews."

"You'll have to write your dad and tell him he has suddenly become a grandfather five times over. I sure wish I could see his face when he reads those lines."

— ❖ —

Mandy, just waking up the next morning, took a moment to figure out where she was. She sat up quickly and then fell back onto her pillow with a small laugh over how hard her heart was pounding.

Until now, she had never thought what it might be like to sleep alone in a bed. Sharing a bed was just a way of life, but as she stretched luxuriously without bumping into anyone she thought how nice this was.

Of course it wasn't bad sleeping with Carrie and Becca—they lay still for the most part and were good cuddlers. But sleeping between Levi and Clovis was another matter. They always woke up in a wrestling match on top of her. Whereupon she would leave the bed in a huff and tell them she would never sleep with them again, not that she ever kept her threat. The next time they were scared or restless she would crawl in between them, always with the intent of returning to her own bed when they were asleep but invariably falling into slumber herself, only to be awakened in the morning by a fist in her middle or a foot in her face.

Actually she'd half expected to wake up and find the entire gang in here with her. They must have slept hard or they surely would have joined her, taking for granted their welcome.

Mandy looked around the wonderful bedroom with a feeling of unreality. Yesterday she woke up in the only house she had ever lived in and remembered instantly that her mother was gone. She wanted so hard to go on as normal and take care of things, but she wondered if it were really possible, even for Becca's sake, to keep up such a front.

The first thing she had done was check her mother's bed. It was empty—the undertaker had seen to that. None of them had slept in it because it felt funny and because there was a slight chance their pa would return. But the bed had not been slept in.

Mandy had been okay until just before lunch when she cried hard, starting everyone's tears. By the time she had them settled enough to have lunch, if you could call it that, she was so tired she wanted to sleep forever.

When the wagon pulled up out front she wasn't afraid of why they'd come, just uncertain, until Pastor Chad's words sent her already foggy mind spinning.

And now this morning.

Mandy pushed out of bed and stepped softly across the floor. She stood in the middle of the rug, so soft beneath her feet, and did a slow circle, attempting to take it all in.

Next to her bed was a table made of a dark, rose-colored wood, the same as the bed, and on the table was an oil lamp made of pink glass. She'd never seen anything like it.

The walk-in closet at the end of the room was spacious and her few items of clothing looked almost lonely on the empty shelves and hooks.

A dresser with a wide mirror above it stood against the wall opposite the closet, but Mandy wasn't interested in her reflection this morning. Her feet, with almost a mind of their own, moved to the place between the two windows where a bookshelf stood.

Mandy went down on her knees before it and simply stared for long minutes. Finally, moving hesitantly as though someone would slap her hand, she reached to lightly touch the books. Her fingers skimmed over the bindings with reverence and something akin to awe.

Amanda Jackson loved to read.

She hadn't always felt that way. With pain she remembered the teacher's dark looks when she struggled long after everyone else her age had understood that mysterious art, despairing of ever catching on and being able to read with the ease of breathing, as her teacher did.

But then one day, very close to her eleventh birthday, it became clear, as though a light had been turned on in her mind. The world of letters, words, and sentences became startlingly clear and Mandy read with a voracious appetite from that moment.

Anyone watching her in the bedroom at the Cameron house this morning, would have been confused by her actions and the tears of joy on her face at just being able to touch these precious volumes. They would have wondered at the way her heart pounded at just the thought of asking Amy if she could read them, hoping she could make her see how careful she would be with each and every one.

Yes, anyone watching her would have been confused unless they understood life in the Jackson household. There had never been enough money for food, let alone anything as extravagant as books, no matter how loved or coveted.

Mandy was startled out of her position on the floor when someone knocked.

"Come in."

"Hi," Amy spoke as she came through the door. "I wasn't sure if you were up. We're about ready to eat."

"I better wake everyone." Mandy spoke uncertainly from her place by the shelves.

"Everyone is downstairs, dressed, and Becca tells me, *starving*." Amy informed her good-naturedly.

"Oh, I'm sorry you had to wait on me."

"Don't apologize, you have time. I just wanted you to know that Silas will be in from the barn in about ten minutes and then we'll be ready to eat."

"Thank you. I'll be right down."

Mandy threw herself into her clothes and rushed down the hall to Carrie's room for the hairbrush. Her hair was thick but not very long, falling only to her shoulders, enabling her to have it brushed and pulled back with a ribbon in a matter of seconds.

Not until she returned the brush to the dresser did she notice how nicely the room was picked up. She walked back down the hall past her own room to the boys' to find it as orderly as the girls', with even the quilt hung perfectly across the bed.

Amy.

While swiftly making her own bed she was amazed to realize she was not jealous of her hostess stepping in to help the kids last night as well as this morning.

Mandy couldn't remember the last time she'd awakened without a list of jobs and duties as long as her arm hanging over her. How nice it felt to have someone else in charge, and Amy seemed to genuinely enjoy it.

Well, she thought as she descended the stairs, best enjoy it, for it certainly won't last.

7

"Father in heaven, I thank you for the beauty of this day and the bounty of this food. Bless us our conversation and surround us with Your love. Amen."

Silas was well aware of the eyes watching him as he served himself some eggs and then passed the bowl to Mandy. The children were a little less hungry this morning, whereas last night their concentration on food had made them much too preoccupied to be aware of a man thanking God for the meal.

The four youngest Jacksons fell on the food with renewed hunger, but Mandy ate a little more cautiously. Silas, watching her surreptitiously, thought she seemed like an animal who had been teased and baited at every meal and forced to beg before being rewarded with food.

He had the feeling that if he suddenly snatched her plate from in front of her, she would accept it docilely as though the few mouthfuls she'd taken were all she deserved.

"I'm headed back out to the barn after breakfast, if anyone would like to come."

"What's in the barn?" Clovis wanted to know.

"Horses." The word was said matter-of-factly, but the response from the boys was the first glimmer of behavior beyond the perfect.

"Horses—did you hear what he said?" The words were shouted. "Can we ride? I know how!"

"You do not, Clovis!"

"I do so, Levi. You just shut your mouth!"

"You shut your own mouth or I'll do it for ya!"

"Oh yeah, just try!"

Mandy was embarrassed over their behavior and had just opened her mouth to shout over them when Silas' voice cut through their words like a whip.

"Boys! That's enough!"

The room was instantly silent. He had not really raised his voice but his deep tone and the authority punctuating every syllable was more than enough to make the boys sit up in their seats, their mouths closed, eyes wide open.

"We will not be riding any horses today." His voice sounded loud in the still room. "And if I don't have your word about not shouting in the barn, you'll not be going. Have I made myself clear?"

"Yes, sir."

"I won't shout in the barn." The words were said in little more than a whisper and came from Rebecca.

"Would you like to go, Becca?"

"Is it just for boys?"

"No, you can come."

Her smile was Silas' thanks and he felt his heart melt in the glow of it. She was the only one of the five that looked as if she'd been fed decently, with her round face and almost pudgy little hands. She shared the same shade of brown hair and hazel eyes with the rest of her family, but the freckles she had were out over her cheeks and not just on her nose.

"I think everyone should go," Amy suggested.

"No," Carrie spoke. "Mandy and I will stay and help clean up."

"I appreciate the offer, girls, but there will be many dishes in the days to come. Go with Silas while he has the time to take you."

Amy's words were still on Mandy's mind as they walked toward the Cameron barn. She made it sound like they were going to be staying for a while and Mandy hadn't expected that. She didn't know what she did expect but this constant barrage of kindness and hospitality was not it.

Maybe her pa would return. He never stayed for very long and any money he had would go toward the bottle he'd enjoy in one of Baxter's bars. It was too much to hope that he would be at the funeral tomorrow.

They had come to the barn and Mandy, deep in her own thoughts, didn't realize Silas was holding the door for her.

"Are you okay?" Silas asked.

"What?"

"You seemed a little far away. If you'd rather not come in, that's fine. Maybe you'd like some time to yourself."

"No, I better stick with the kids. They don't always obey Carrie."

"Maybe not Carrie, but I don't think I'll have any trouble." Silas said this with a smile and Mandy actually smiled back at the big man.

Why she's lovely! he thought in honest surprise.

But the smile disappeared as quickly as it had appeared and her question told him where her thoughts had been. "Do you think the sheriff will find my pa?"

"I don't know, Mandy. I'm praying he will."

Mandy moved into the barn then, her thoughts in confusion over her host's last statement.

8

"Luke, I thought you were going to the barn."

"I am, but Si took the Jackson kids out there and I wanted him to have some time with them. Hey, Christine. Do me a favor and give me their names again."

"Okay, let's see—Mandy, Carrie, Levi, Clovis...or is it Clovis, Levi...well anyhow, then Rebecca."

"Mandy, Carrie, Levi, Clovis, Rebecca?"

"That's it, I believe."

Luke let out a low whistle and shook his head. "That's quite a family to acquire overnight. Sometimes I think I won't hold up with two."

"Yes, who would have thought when Pastor Nolan came to Gram's yesterday it was to tell all of us that Si had just taken the Jackson children home for an indefinite period of time."

"It was a surprise. But if anyone can handle it, Si and Amy can. I've never seen a couple so ready for children of their own."

"Speaking of children—what do you mean you can barely hold up with two? How about three?" Christine's hands went to her hips and Luke smiled at the movement for it made her very pregnant stomach stick out that much farther.

"Oh, I'll love three."

"As much as you love the first two?"

"Yep."

"As much as you love their mother?"

"No-o-o, I don't love their mother. I just keep her around to cook and clean."

"Luke Cameron!" Christine cried in outrage as she swung a dishcloth at him. He sidestepped it easily and kissed her cheek on the way by. But the teasing smile fell from his face the instant he saw the tears in her eyes.

"Christie, you know I don't mean it." His voice was repentant, all teasing gone.

"I know," she sniffed, "but when I'm pregnant—"

"You cry all the time," he finished for her and put his arms around her. "Forgive me, I won't tease you again."

"You probably will and I'll cry all over again and you'll be sorry and I'll..."

"Have I been that bad?" Luke asked.

"No, I'm just—"

"Pregnant." He finished for her one last time and they both laughed. Luke looked out the window then and saw Silas leaving the barn.

"You sure you're okay?"

"Umm hmm."

"Okay, I'm headed out now." He kissed her lingeringly and looked into her eyes to gauge how she really was. "If you need me, send Josh."

"Well, how was the barn?"

"Big." Mandy and Carrie answered in unison and Amy laughed.

Both girls used the washbasin without prompting, and Mandy went to the bread dough waiting to be kneaded. Carrie picked up a wet skillet and a drying towel.

"Where are Becca and the boys?"

"Silas was showing them the swings in that big tree."

Amy knew the place of course. Most of the trees on the Cameron acres were bunched together, such as the oaks near their house, but there was one oak, a real beauty, that stood alone by the barn. From it hung two swings with thick ropes and wide wood seats that let a person soar with the birds if they could pump that high.

Amy stepped to the back porch off the kitchen, and could see Levi and Clovis already high in the air with each forward thrust of their legs.

"Will they let Becca have a turn?" Amy called through the door as she watched the little girl at the trunk of the tree.

"Not unless they're told to." Amy heard Mandy say as she reentered the house.

"Amy, do you always bake this much bread?" Carrie questioned as she joined Mandy over the dough.

"No, the extra is for tomorrow."

The girls both looked blank.

"Oh no, didn't my uncle tell you there's a light lunch planned after the funeral? It's to be at Silas' grandmother's."

"No," Mandy's voice was small.

"I'm sorry he forgot. If you'd rather not we can cancel. Whatever you're the most comfortable with."

"It's not that we're uncomfortable, it's just that this is so much food and—" Mandy's voice trailed off.

"What Mandy is trying to say is we didn't get out much, and well, there probably won't be very many people there."

Amy's nails dug into her palm as her fist clenched beneath the folds of her skirt. They were so accepting of not having anyone care, just as long as no one was put out by having prepared too much food or anything.

"Mandy—Carrie—I hope I can say this right." Amy spoke slowly, weighing her words.

"For however short or long a time you stay here with us, you are family. Even if you were to leave today, the five of you would always be thought of as family by me, and I know Silas feels the same way. And if you're in our family, it automatically makes you part of the whole Cameron family. They're a big group, all of whom are planning to be there tomorrow."

"How many are in Silas' family?" Mandy looked a little uncertain.

"Luke raises horses with Silas and he's married to Christine. They have Josh and Kate, and Christine is pregnant. Luke has a twin brother who lives in town. His name is

Mark, and he is Baxter's doctor. He and his wife, Susanne, have four little girls—Emily, Elizabeth, Ellen, and Erika.

"Silas was born after Luke and Mark, and the three of them have a sister, Julia. She's married to John MacDonald, 'Mac' for short, and they have Calvin, Charles, and Robyn. The youngest is Paul, and he lives up in Bayfield, Wisconsin. You won't meet them now, but Paul's wife is Abigail and they have twin girls, Jessica and Julie, and a baby boy, Timothy."

"How many was that?"

"With Paul's family not being here and counting Silas' Grandma Em, there will be over 20 of us. And don't forget that your family has lived in this town a long time. I'm sure there will be friends and acquaintances of your mother and father of whom you're not even aware."

Both girls nodded and Carrie smiled at her before they bent back over the bowl. Amy, thinking they might want to talk in privacy, said she was going out to see that Becca got a turn on the swing. She'd have been surprised to know that neither of the girls felt like talking after she left.

9

"Grandma Em?" Ross Beckett called out as he opened the front door. "Are you in?"

"Ross!" Grandma Em spoke the name with obvious pleasure as she came down the stairs and into the parlor. He bent and kissed her weathered cheek and then hugged her closely as if she really were his grandmother.

"How was your trip to Hayward?"

"Great!"

"And your parents?"

"They're fine. You'd think I'd set up my law practice in Baxter years ago, the way my mother cried."

"Maybe she saw changes in you."

"She said as much. My dad always attributes it to my getting older. I hope one of these days he'll see God in my life and realize *He* is making the changes."

"You know Ross," she spoke as they took seats on the elegant living room furniture, "maybe he does see God in you and doesn't know how to respond to the man you've become."

He looked at her without comment, then across the room at nothing in particular.

"Have you eaten?" She finally broke into his pensive mood.

"No, actually I haven't."

"Well, come along then. I'll feed you and bring you up to date on the news in town. The very latest of which is that Silas and Amy have five children."

"What!"

"You heard me right. Sit down and I'll explain."

— ✤ —

Shortly after lunch at the Silas Cameron home, the women of the house, Amy on down to Rebecca, stood in serious discussion in Mandy's room.

"I think I'm the only one who has a black dress that fits."

"Alright Carrie, why don't you go and get it, and we'll make sure it's pressed and ready for tomorrow."

"I have one of Mama's."

Carrie stopped on her way out of the room. "Don't believe her, Amy. The dress Mandy's talking about is terrible on her."

"Hush, Carrie." The words were spoken more in tired resignation than anger.

"No, I won't hush. We could fit two of you in that dress and you know it."

"Well that's just too bad, because I'm not wearing anything but black to Mama's service and that's that."

Amy could see Carrie was going to continue to argue the point. It was time she stepped in.

"Carrie, please go ahead and get your dress and Becca's, too, the brown one you said would fit this winter. I have a dress Mandy can wear."

"I need a black dress, too."

"I'm sorry, Becca, but I don't have one your size. I think your brown dress will be just fine. Carrie is bringing it and I'll get it pressed and all ready for you."

The little girl didn't look convinced, and Amy held her breath waiting for a top-of-her-voice objection. Blessedly, Carrie returned in only a few seconds and Amy was on her knees in front of Becca trying the dress on her.

The fabric was far from new, but the original seams were still in very good shape and the dress wasn't as roomy in the body as Amy had been expecting. Even the length would do for the few hours she would be in it.

Amy concentrated on buttoning the dress and then praised her littlest houseguest on how nicely the dress fit, as though Rebecca herself had something to do with the growing of her body.

They checked the boys' things before heading downstairs to Amy's room where she pulled a black dress from the closet and laid it across the bed.

"Why don't you stay in here, Mandy, and try this on? I'll go to the kitchen and put the irons on the stove. Come out when you're ready." Amy exited, taking Mandy's sisters with her, praying as she went that the dress would be suitable.

Mandy heard the door close but didn't move from her place. She hadn't been in this room before, and even though she was not surprised to find it as lovely as the rest of the house, she still felt like standing and taking it all in.

The bed was quite big, she decided. No, *grand* was a better word. The headboard was towering and ornate, and though the bed was not very wide it was extremely long to the foot. The woods of the bedroom furniture were not consistent, but it didn't detract in any way from the dark green decor. The bed itself was dark walnut, as were the small tables on either side of the bed. The small wardrobe and writing desk under the window were pine.

Mandy spotted an open book on the desk and looked no further. She had to restrain herself from picking it up to read. She did move closer though and saw instantly it was a Bible, opened to the book of John. Mandy had read the Bible a few times at the schoolhouse, enjoying as always the sensation of seeing words with recognition. But each time she read it she went away with a thirsty feeling, a feeling of not quite understanding all she'd read. Most times Mandy assumed that a person had to be very smart to understand the Bible and that she had never reached that level of intelligence.

When she finally turned to the task of dressing she did so quickly, with little thought as to how she might look. In the corner stood a full-length mirror. Mandy stepped in front of it with the intent of taking a quick peek. She knew if she dawdled overly long Amy would have to go to the bother of looking for her. They were all being trouble enough.

Unexpectedly her own reflection stopped all haste. Never before had she worn a dress that fit her so well. It was just slightly loose at the waist, but the length and shoulder cuts were perfect. Mandy's eyes traveled to her flat chest. Amy was not what you would consider full-figured, but Mandy without a spare inch of flesh anywhere on her, including her breasts, found herself wishing that her body filled out that part of the dress a little more, like Amy's did.

"Does it fit? Wow, Mandy!" The question and exclamation both came from Carrie, who popped her head in the bedroom door.

"Does it look okay?"

"Yeah, it looks really nice. I think the nicest you've ever looked."

"I'm glad. I wonder if Mama would be pleased."

"She would be Mandy. Mama always wanted more for us than she could give. Mandy, is that why we came here, because you thought Mama would want it?"

"Yes, that's part of the reason. I mean, I couldn't stand the thought of us all being separated."

"Yeah, that would be awful. What's the other reason?"

She thought for a moment. "I don't know if I can put it into words. It was just like I *had* to accept Silas' offer, almost like something inside of me wouldn't let me say no. Does that make any sense?"

"I think so. Anyway, I'm glad you did. I think our house is scary without Mama there and who knows when Pa will be back."

"Amy wants to know if she needs to press your dress, Mandy, or abust the hem," Becca interrupted from the doorway.

"I think she means adjust the hem, Becca."

"Yeah, adjust the hem."

"Please tell her we're coming."

Becca, preening with importance, skipped back out of the room to deliver the message.

10

Mandy could not tear her eyes off the plain pine box that held her mother's body. It was all so final. It didn't matter to her that the burial was taking place on the poor side of the cemetery, the side where the weeds grew high and no one could afford engraved stones or monuments. All that mattered was that her mother was gone. *Gone*. The word seemed to choke the breath from her and she groped for her sister's hand, not even noticing a hand much larger than Carrie's covered hers and held it tight.

Ross felt his throat clog upon the contact, something he had not expected. He knew very well that she had meant to reach for her sister but in her grief, he was sure, she reached to her left and he was there. There was no thought or hesitation, she reached and he responded, taking her small, cold, very thin hand in his own. He wasn't even sure why he had ended up standing so close to her, but when everyone had gathered around the gravesite, next to the Jackson children was where he found himself.

Not that anyone else in the circle knew them any better than he did, with the exception of Silas and Amy, or so Grandma Em had explained. They were so new to the group and the circumstances that brought them into the family so painful. It certainly wasn't expected of Silas to parade them around for introductions.

Pastor Nolan spoke words of comfort and hope, but Ross sincerely doubted if anything he said would alleviate the look of hopelessness he read on Amanda Jackson's face.

The casket was now being lowered into the ground and he felt a tremor run through her. Ross caught movement out of the corner of his eye, as Amanda's sister turned to cling to her oldest sibling. It wasn't until the moment she dropped his hand that he was certain she hadn't even been aware of holding it.

Carrie and Mandy clung to one another, vaguely aware of Rebecca in Amy's arms and Silas with the boys. *She's really gone and we're alone.* The words wouldn't stop screaming inside Mandy's head.

It was customary for the family of the deceased to throw handfuls of dirt on top of the casket but none of the Jackson children were aware of this or would have done so, even if they had been. The burying of their mother was something that had to be done, but they wanted nothing to do, even symbolically, with the actual act.

Silas sensed a need to remove his adopted family from the gravesite. Amy moved to stand near the boys, Becca's arms around her neck, while Silas came up behind Mandy and Carrie.

"We can go now if you'd like."

"Can we really?" Mandy whispered. "We don't need to stay until everyone is gone?"

"No, everyone knows you're hurting. Ross will take you to the wagon. Amy and I will be right behind you."

Silas had flicked a glance at Ross as he'd said the words and no other action was necessary. Silas turned them gently from the grave and Ross immediately stepped over and put his hand beneath Mandy's elbow. Neither she nor Carrie seemed to really be aware of him.

He'd just lifted Carrie to the rear seat beside Mandy when Aaron Marks, one of Baxter's businessmen, stepped up to Mandy's side of the wagon.

"I'm sorry Miss Jackson. I won't be coming to Mrs. Cameron's, but I wanted to express my sympathy. I never met your mother, but your father and I have had business dealings."

"You know our pa?" At the mention of her father, Mandy became instantly attentive to the portly, ruddy-faced man.

"Yes I do, though I admit I haven't seen him for a spell."

"He's been away."

"You wouldn't have heard from him by chance, would you?" The question was stated with casual aplomb.

"Just a letter to Mama earlier, during the winter."

"Ah. Well, I'll be off now." He departed rather swiftly, without acknowledgement to Ross or anyone else who was now aboard the full wagon. Ross and Silas exchanged a brief look over Marks' odd behavior, but no one observed it as Silas put the team into motion.

Mandy was a little disappointed that Mr. Marks had mentioned her pa without any news of his whereabouts. The letter, she remembered, was at least six months old, and though she'd never read it her mother had said he was out west somewhere. Mandy realized that she'd forgotten the small bundle of papers in her mother's dresser. She decided to walk home tomorrow and get them. Maybe she should leave a note for Pa while she was there.

An hour later Ross left Grandma Em's crowded parlor and headed out the kitchen door to the back porch steps. Rebecca, Clovis, and Levi, all on the top step, slid over to let him pass. Ross stepped by them, but rather than going into the backyard, sank down onto the second step and turned to face them.

"Hi," Clovis said.

"Hi," Ross responded as he watched Rebecca struggle to hold her plate and drink her lemonade at the same time. He rescued the plate and then traded her when she'd slacked her thirst.

"Don't drink it." Becca told him seriously when he took a moment too long placing it beside her.

"Oh, Becca, he's not gonna drink your old juice. Don't be so dumb." Levi stated with his usual impatience for his family.

"She's just dumb," he said to Ross.

"Oh, I don't think she's dumb," he said mildly. "After all, she doesn't know me and I might have drunk from her cup."

"You like lemonade?" Clovis wanted to know.

"Mm hmm."

"You can have some of mine." Clovis' was naturally generous.

"Thank you, Clovis, but I've had mine."

"How'd you know his name?" Levi wanted to know.

"Grandma Em told me."

"She's that old lady that lives here, huh?"

"She is Silas' grandmother. And yes, this is her house." Ross tempered the remark about "that old lady." Grandma Em was old, but Ross never thought of her that way. It somehow seemed disrespectful.

"Do you know my name?" The voice was muffled around a cookie.

"You must be Rebecca, or do you like Becky?"

"Becca," Levi answered for her. "I'll bet ya don't know my name."

"Levi."

The ten-year-old looked impressed and Ross smiled.

"What's your name?"

"Ross."

"Did you know our mama?"

"No, I wish I had."

"She got sick and died."

"Mandy got sick last year." Becca chimed in as though talking about the weather.

"Yeah, she got all hot with a fever and Mama cut all her hair off. She cried. Girls are dumb about their hair."

Ross easily pictured Amanda's short hair, just brushing her shoulders and pulled back at the sides. Even though he'd not given any prior thought to it, he realized it did stand out in a day when women and girls alike rarely cut their hair.

"Are you being careful with those plates and cups?"

The kids answered their sister affirmatively. Ross, stuck in his daydream, had a hard time figuring out if Mandy was really standing there. She had come around the side of the house, and his imagination was still at work. He must have stared for quite a few seconds because she finally said, "I just can't remember. I'm sorry."

"What?"

"Your name," the words came out in embarrassment. "You were waiting for me to remember your name, but with so many people today and, well—"

Ross came off the step in a single fluid movement. "I should be the one apologizing for staring rudely. And my name is Ross, Ross Beckett."

"I remember now. You're a lawyer here in town."

"That's right," he said with a smile.

"But now I've forgotten how you're related to Silas' grandmother."

"I'm not. That is, not by blood. I'm a friend of another of her grandsons—Paul. He and his wife and family live farther north, as did I until January."

They seemed to run out of words but Mandy was saved from an awkward moment when Rebecca needed her. Ross, watching her turn to her sister, felt something akin to pain when she passed close enough for him to see that her eyes were red from crying. The strangest feeling came over him, and he felt a strong urge to hold her hand again, an urge he wondered about for the rest of the day.

11

"Thank you for coming." Carrie wondered if she would remember any of these people's names as they filed out of Grandma Em's. She wished she'd gone with Mandy to check on the kids.

"Yes, I'm Carrie. Rebecca is younger."

"Yes, she was a good mother. Thank you."

"No, we haven't talked to our pa yet."

"I'm 14."

Carrie was beginning to feel like she wanted to cry again. She knew they were all being kind, but she wanted to be left alone. And her throat hurt. Badly.

"Carrie, I didn't realize you were here at the door by yourself. Why don't you come and sit down." Amy spoke softly as she approached.

"That woman, I don't know her name, said she was leaving and that I should see her to the door. And then it seemed like everyone else decided to leave at the same time and well..." The 14-year-old's eyes filled with tears and Amy immediately led her to the kitchen.

Wordlessly she pulled out a chair for Carrie at the table and poured her a glass of water. Amy watched her drink.

"What's the matter, Carrie?"

"What do you mean?"

"You're swallowing funny."

"My throat hurts a little."

Amy reached out and laid a cool hand on Carrie's flushed cheek. "Your skin is warm. How long has your throat hurt?"

"I don't know. I'm okay."

"Well, I think Mark had best have a look." Amy wasn't gone from the room more than a second before Carrie bolted for the back door.

"Carrie, what's your hurry?" Mandy asked her sister as she came back down the back porch steps so fast she nearly stepped on Rebecca.

"No hurry," she tried for nonchalance but Mandy wasn't convinced. She could tell Carrie was upset but knew that here and now was not the time to question her.

Confusion set in a few moments later when the back door opened once again for Silas and Mark. Carrie, upon seeing them, darted around a silent Ross to hide behind Mandy.

"Tell Silas I'm not sick, Mandy, please." The last word was desperately whispered. Mandy stared up at the men in befuddlement and Silas spoke.

"Carrie, Amy said your throat hurt. Is that right?"

Carrie did not immediately answer and the boys, taking it all in from their vantage point on the step, rose and went to flank their oldest sister.

The scene was piteous with the four of them standing together. Amy, watching from the kitchen window, felt her throat contract and wished she'd kept her mouth shut.

"I think Carrie's okay." Mandy broke the awkward silence.

"Yes, I'm fine," Carrie reluctantly answered over Mandy's shoulder in a voice that to everyone's ears, including her own, sounded hoarse.

Both Silas and Mark carefully approached the small group. Ross, sensing he was not needed, scooped an unresisting Becca off the step and went inside.

"I certainly messed that up," Ross heard Amy say once he and Becca were inside.

"It's alright, Amy," Susanne comforted her. She too had watched the scene from the kitchen. "You're naturally concerned for her. She looked terrified, didn't she?" Tears standing in Susanne's eyes started Amy's. Ross busied himself with Becca's sticky hands and face. Thanking God as he did so that she had not demanded to be left with her sister.

"Ross, did Carrie say anything when she came out?"

"No, but it was obvious she was upset. She looks a little pale to me. But then they all do, and I don't wonder, considering the day they've had."

"Well, I think I'll rescue Gram from the kids, since we're the last ones to leave," Susanne said. "I'll be praying for all of you, Amy. Please tell Mark I went on home." The two women embraced, and Amy turned to find Becca reaching for another cookie. She gave her a carrot stick instead and although Becca frowned at the vegetable in her hand, she ate it.

"You're doing fine, you know."

Amy simply stared at Ross, tears still wet on her lashes, as he spoke to her.

"I mean it. I was watching you earlier and you handle them all very lovingly; they couldn't ask for more."

"Oh, I don't know, Ross. Sometimes I think I've bit off more than I can chew, and it's only been since Sunday. I just want to do the right thing."

"And you're doing that. There was no way you could know that Carrie was going to panic over seeing Mark."

"Yes, you're right about that. By the way, you don't do so badly with children yourself." She nodded toward the wet dishcloth in his hand.

Laughing softly before answering, Ross tossed the cloth back into the dishpan. "Just recently, in the last two years or so, I began to take an interest in my sister's kids. They're a very destructive bunch and that's on a good day. You learn a lot quickly in order to survive."

"How many does she have?"

"Six."

"Your folks must love it."

"Well actually no, they don't think it's all that great. Gwen married a man my folks did not approve of. She and Stan live about 40 miles away. My folks take advantage of the distance to not see them more than once a year.

"Not until I became a Christian did I realize that their attitude toward my brother-in-law was wrong. And now that I know him a little better, I think he's a pretty decent guy. He loves my sister to distraction, I'll say that much for him, and he's also more receptive to the gospel than anyone else in my family."

"How was your trip? Were you able to see your sister?"

"Yes, I saw her. She's doing fine, as are my folks."

"How's Sarah?" When Ross didn't immediately answer, Amy apologized. "I'm sorry Ross if I'm out of line. I just assumed things were pretty serious between the two of you."

"Yes, actually they are. But Sarah doesn't want to move away from Hayward, and I know God wants me in Baxter. As you can see, we are at an impasse."

"I'll be remembering you both in my prayers, Ross."

"Thanks, Amy. And you, Rebecca Jackson, are a wiggle worm." Ross had been holding Becca in his lap as they talked, only to find that she shifted every few seconds. He set her on her feet but she leaned against his legs, seeming in no hurry to be separated from him.

"Well, Ross, I see you have a new friend." Grandma Em spoke from the doorway. "I came in to see if anyone could tell me what was going on in the backyard with Silas and Mark."

"We're not sure ourselves. Carrie has a sore throat and I overreacted. I'm afraid I scared Carrie by rushing off to get Mark."

"I'll wait with you if you don't mind, just in case I'm needed. Come here Rebecca and see your great-grandma."

12

"Carrie, did anyone tell you when you met Mark that he's a doctor?" Silas asked the question as though there was nothing unusual about the way Carrie was cowering behind her sister or the way the boys flanked Mandy in a protective stance.

"Yes, I know he's a doctor. But my throat's okay."

"Is it really, honey?" Silas' voice was extremely sensitive, showing just how much he cared for the welfare of this girl.

Carrie had never heard a man speak in this way and she felt her resistance melting. She wasn't afraid of the doctor so much as afraid of being sick. Her young heart was bruised with the loss of her mother, and she couldn't stop herself from wondering if she was going to get sick and die too.

Silas and Mark stood together and watched Carrie struggle. They saw tears fill her eyes before she bent forward to rest her head on Mandy's shoulder. The movement sparked Mandy into motion.

"You boys go into the house and check on Becca. And don't touch anything."

They looked for a long moment at Mark. Finally Mandy gave them a little push. "We'll be fine."

They obeyed then and Mandy gave Carrie her full attention. "You can't really believe he's going to hurt you. What's the matter?"

"I'm not sick."

"Even if you are, Carrie, you're not going to die." The young woman spoke the words with such startling clarity that Mark and Silas were surprised, having thought of it but figuring it would be in some way harmful to the tender emotions of this young family to mention it. It was the first experience they were to have with the honest straightforwardness of Amanda Jackson.

The tears that had just been standing in Carrie's eyes coursed down her cheeks. Mandy pulled her gently into her arms. They were very close in height and frame, but anyone could see that for Carrie, Mandy was a lifeline.

"Come into the house, Carrie, and let Dr. Cameron look at you," her big sister urged. "He's got four girls of his own. He'll know what to do." Mandy wasn't sure if the words would be any comfort, but she'd never seen Carrie like this and honestly didn't know what to do. Of course they were all going to act differently these days with everything familiar behind them.

"Actually my bag is over at my office," Mark spoke for the first time. "Would you mind coming over there, Carrie?"

"If Mandy can come."

"Certainly."

"Maybe I better check on the kids before we go."

"I'll do that," Silas offered. "You go ahead. We'll come by in a bit and pick you up on our way out of town."

Mandy and Carrie followed the tall frame of Mark Cameron down the street to a white two-story home that was the private residence as well as the office of Baxter's doctor. They had seen it from the outside and knew whose home it was. But there had never been any money to pay a doctor, so the front yard with its flowers and curtains showing in every window, was as close as they'd ever come to the inside of the doctor's office.

Money, Mandy thought. *We haven't any. I'll have to say something.*

"Dr. Cameron, I—"

"That's Uncle Mark to you, remember."

"Oh, that's right. Well, anyhow, we can't pay you for this. I mean, thank you for offering to check Carrie, but we haven't any money and she's probably fine. We've had a lot of changes in a short time and that might be getting us down."

Mark stood a moment and looked into the faces of these two young women. His mind was instantly transported back to similar confrontations with his sister-in-law, Christine.

Only then she wasn't his sister-in-law. She was Christine Bennett and she was bound and determined not to be beholding to anyone.

But this was different. This girl stated their financial situation with startling honesty, even at the risk, no, *expectation*, that they would be sent away without help.

Mark spoke in that gentle voice that the girls were coming to recognize as a hallmark of the Cameron men. "I never charge my nieces or nephews for my services."

He gave them a moment to let the words soak in and then told Carrie to take a seat on the examination table. She did so hesitantly, and with long, strong fingers probing along the side of her jaw, Mark began his examination.

"Well, Carrie," he spoke after a long, thorough look at her throat, "everything is pretty red in there and I imagine quite sore. I've got something I want you to gargle with, and then I want to see you again tomorrow. As for the rest of the day, I want you to rest and only eat things that are easy to swallow. Amy will know what to fix."

"Thank you, Doctor, but I'm not—"

"Uncle Mark."

"Thank you, Uncle Mark, but I'm not sure I can come back into town tomorrow." Mark stared at Carrie for a moment. He wondered how long it would be before they saw that Silas and Amy thought of them as their very own.

"Carrie, if you needed to go back East right now for anything that would help you, Silas would have you aboard the train this afternoon. He'll get you here tomorrow."

The heartwarming, sincerely spoken words brought smiles to Mandy's and Carrie's lips, lighting their beautiful hazel eyes and showing rows of white straight teeth, and giving Mark the same glimpse of loveliness that Silas had witnessed in Mandy.

Mercy, he thought, *these girls could be heartbreakers without even trying.*

Carrie was off the table now and Mark disappeared into a closetlike room to mix the medicine he'd prescribed. He was just finishing up when Silas knocked on the door. Explaining his findings to Silas, Mark saw the three out to the wagon, with what he hoped was some peace of mind.

Sue was waiting in the office when he returned. "How is Carrie?"

"Nothing serious, but I'm going to keep an eye on her."

"She and Mandy are awfully sweet, aren't they?"

"Yes they are. I've an inkling the young men at church are going to find the pew that Silas and Amy usually sit in a lot more interesting from now on."

13

"I'm sorry you don't feel well." Amy spoke quietly as she settled next to Carrie.

Carrie looked at her from her place on the sofa in the living room. Silas had insisted, as soon as they'd arrived home, that she rest there.

"You don't want to be up in the bedroom all by yourself," he said as he'd carried blankets and pillows from his bedroom. "Just take your shoes off and get comfortable right here."

Carrie had glanced at Amy as if to ask permission, but Amy had only smiled at her and said she had just the thing for a sore throat. She was back in less than 15 minutes with a steaming cup and sat beside Carrie as she drank. Silas had taken the boys out to the barn with him and Mandy had Becca upstairs in hopes of getting her to take a much-needed nap.

"Do you have a headache or anything, Carrie?"

"No, it's just my throat," Carrie said, and already half the cup was gone.

"Well, it could be the start of something worse, so I'm glad Mark is taking care of you."

"What is this I'm drinking?"

"It was a recipe my mother used. She always gave it to me when I was sick."

"Does your mother live around here?"

"No, Carrie, she doesn't. I haven't had a chance to tell you, but my mother died when I was 14."

Carrie looked stricken but didn't apologize for asking. "I'm 14."

"Yes, I know. It isn't easy is it?"

"It's awful." Her voice shook but tears did not come. "Is your pa gone, too?"

"No, he lives in Neillsville where I grew up."

Carrie nodded and said nothing more.

"I think it might be a good idea if you rested your throat, Carrie. I'll be in the kitchen if you need anything."

"Amy," Carrie called, causing Amy to turn expectantly before she could leave the room. "Thank you."

"You're welcome, sweetheart."

— ✛ —

"Do you have a favorite?"

"Mm hmm. Guess which one."

The boys had no trouble. Titan, the tremendous black stallion whose name they had seen on his stable door, tossed his head and flicked his tail as if he knew he was the topic of conversation and praise. He raced around the small corral in display and stopped to call to four mares in the field beyond his own fence.

"I don't suppose we'll ever get to ride him." Levi's voice was too cynical for his years.

"Well, I wouldn't go so far as to say never, but he's not a pony, that's for certain. There are other horses here you can ride."

"Today?" They chorused together.

"Sure." His answer surprised them into momentary silence, a silence they made up for when, seconds later, yells of excitement erupted from them, causing the high-spirited Titan's front hooves to dance in the air and his eyes to roll back in fear.

Silas led the boys into the barn, knowing that a talk about their conduct around the stables was in order before he set them on the back of any horse, no matter how docile.

— ✛ —

"I'm not sleepy, Mandy, really." The five-year-old's argument was accompanied by a yawn, and Mandy only shook her head at her sister's stubbornness.

"You don't have to go to sleep, Becca, but you do have to rest, *with* your eyes closed."

Becca gave in then with lots of sighing and turning from one side to the next. Lying next to her, Mandy was just drowsy enough not to care how much she moved as long as she could rest herself and let her mind drift.

The first place it stopped was Carrie. Poor thing. She was never sick and then to come down with something on the day of Mama's funeral, well, it was the worst kind of luck. At least Mark Cameron hadn't expected payment for his services. She would have hated to leave, but there just wasn't any money so there would have been no choice.

The next face her mind conjured up was that of Ross Beckett. He was far and away the nicest man of her own age she'd ever met. He was nice looking too. He wasn't as tall as all the Cameron men, but then not many men were. She guessed him to be about six foot, which was a good nine inches over the top of her own head. But it wasn't his height that made him stand out in her mind, or the sandy brown hair that fell over his forehead when his hat was off. Or even the color of his eyes, such a soft blue.

No, it wasn't any of those things. It was the way he paid attention to what you were saying. Not just heard but listened, making you feel as though what you were saying, no matter how simple or inane, was the most important thing in the world at that moment.

Mandy had watched him in the short time they talked, before Carrie came out. Especially the way he handled Levi, Clovis, and Becca. He talked to them like adults but his hand was close, even when she stood there, to help . . .

His hand.

"I held his hand." Mandy spoke the words aloud. As she remembered his hand closing over hers, Mandy felt the blood rushing to her cheeks, not in embarrassment but something else, something she couldn't define.

What a comfort it had been, she realized suddenly. Reaching and finding that big, warm hand had been exactly what she needed to get her through that moment at her mother's grave. She would have to thank him when she saw him again. *If* she saw him again, she amended, even as she hoped she would.

So wrapped up in her thoughts, Mandy had not realized that Becca had finally fallen asleep.

"I really should get up and do something to help Amy." But Mandy's eyes were drifting shut; her body had other ideas.

Her last thought before she drifted off to sleep was getting her mother's papers and leaving a note for her pa. She'd have to discuss it with Amy...

Aaron Marks stood at his office window overlooking Baxter's main street and reread the letter in his hand. He withdrew a match from his pocket to light his cigar. The smoke curled around his head as he once again read the last line. "I'll be home this summer and it'll be different this time, I promise."

He raised both cigar and letter but changed his mind and pulled back short of lighting the paper. Walking to the cabinet where he kept his files, he reached in until he felt the false back. It moved easily under his touch, and the paper disappeared inside.

He scowled at the wall, where music suddenly sprang to life from the bar next door, and clamped the cigar tight in his teeth. The last thing he needed was music when he had to decide what move to make next. The din grew steadily louder, a little too raucous for so early in the day.

He reached for his jacket and started toward the door. There just might be something interesting going on right now. One never knew what one could learn from the patrons of the bar.

14

A strand of hair kept slipping down into Amy's face, and she blew it out of the way for what felt like the hundredth time.

"You sound like a billows," Silas teased her as he came in from the yard. His shadows, Levi and Clovis, right behind him.

Her laugh was a little breathless as she leaned into the laundry tub.

"My turn, Amy," exclaimed Mandy as she came in from the dining area with a basket of clothes in her arms.

"Mandy, you're just in time. My arms are getting tired."

"I was talking with Carrie. She feels guilty that she's not out here working. So I used one of your lines, Amy, 'there will be plenty of laundry in the days to come.'"

"Good thinking. I'll take this basket out to the line and then be right back with you."

Silas scooped up the basket before Amy could touch it and stood waiting, as ever her faithful servant. Amy gave him her prettiest smile and sailed out the door, very much a woman in love. Mandy watched them with an unreadable expression before plunging her hands into the soapy tub.

Amy's hands flew as she filled out the clothesline and Silas stood holding the basket as she moved along briskly with clothes pins in her mouth. At one point, when her mouth was empty, he bent so he could kiss her, as she retrieved a pillow slip from the basket. She wholeheartedly returned the kiss, unaware of Levi and Clovis in close attention.

"I love you, Si Cameron," Amy spoke quietly.

"The feeling is quite mutual, I assure you."

Amy became aware of the boys just then, and Silas felt her stiffen. His voice came for her ears alone. "They're going to see us as a man and woman in love, sweetheart. Don't pull away from me."

"I just didn't realize they'd followed you, I'm not really embarrassed, just surprised."

"No more time alone." He raised his voice to a normal level then. "We'll get out of your hair and leave you to your work. I'm going over to Luke's and then into town. While Carrie is seeing Mark, the boys and I will have time to go to the store if you want to make a list. Tell Carrie I'll be about a half hour, and to please be ready."

"Well, Carrie, how does it feel?"

"It's still sore but not as bad."

"You had a good night's sleep?"

Carrie nodded and looked so surprised that Mark smiled. Oh, to be young again and without worry. He'd bet Silas had been up to check on her more than once.

"Let's have a look."

Clovis, who had decided to stay with his sister, leaned close as he watched the doctor look into her mouth.

"Does it hurt, Carrie?"

She couldn't answer, but Mark noticed Clovis move closer and touch his sister's arm. Again Mark's examination was gentle and thorough.

"Your jaw was a little swollen yesterday, but there's no swelling today. And the throat isn't quite so inflamed. I think we'll keep up with the gargling and unless you get a fever or start to feel much worse, I'll see you in a week."

"Thank you. Come on Clovis. We'll wait for Silas out front."

"Oh, there's no need for that. Come on through to the house. Sue and the girls will want to see you." Carrie, still a little fearful of this man, followed slowly. Clovis, knowing that the doctor had kids to play with, skipped along without hesitation.

Baxter's newest businessman, Ross Beckett, stayed seated behind his desk even though his customer was exiting. Aaron Marks. What was it about the man that rubbed him the wrong way? Ross considered himself a public servant and as yet, had never turned anyone away, but even though Marks' request had been innocent enough, Ross felt hesitant, as though helping him was going to harm someone else.

He made some notes about the land on which Aaron Marks wanted confirmation and then turned back to his letter to Sarah. He reread what he had written, wanting it to be just right. He planned to post it that day.

Dear Sarah,

I hated leaving when things between us were so unsettled, but I had to get back. My trip was a good one, but you were not far from my thoughts and I felt pained at every mile that separated us.

I know now that compromise is what is needed here, on both our parts. But there is one thing about which I cannot compromise, and that is living in Baxter. Sarah, this is where God wants me.

Baxter is not a "hick" town. Even though you refused me adamantly while I was there, will you please reconsider coming here for a visit? I'll be moving to my new place in a few weeks and Grandma Em would be thrilled to have you stay with her.

I know you would love the people here, and they would love you. The church is wonderful. It has a spirit of loving welcome for everyone who walks through the door.

I realize Baxter is far from home, but we could visit as often as we're able. After all, my family is in Hayward too.

I want very much to be sensitive to your needs, but I still wish you would come my way a little. I'm trying to do what's right for both of us and for our life together, if it is in fact, God's will.

Know that I'll be praying for you as you read this and reply. Give my love to your family. I miss you.

Love, Ross

— ✛ —

Ross set the paper aside and leaned his elbows on the desk. His gaze fell on his door where the glass read:

Ross Beckett
Attorney at Law

How knowledgeable I am, he thought, when it comes to the law. Pages memorized out of books, hours spent with a seasoned lawyer who practiced up north—gleaning from him, learning, soaking it all in, to be the best at my job. But this—

Ross' mind stopped there. Matters of the head were so much easier than matters of the heart. It wasn't as though his heart was never involved. There were heartbreaking cases, like a woman from the Hayward area, widowed a few days, coming to him and wanting to sell her land and farm. She still bore the bruises of the last beating her husband had given her before he fell down the stairs in a drunken stupor. She couldn't wait to sell and get out of the area; the sooner the better. Ross had asked her if maybe she'd want to wait and give herself some time. But she informed him in a firm voice that she'd had plenty of time, 30 years of time, to be exact.

Oh yes, his heart was sometimes involved, more than it should be. But nothing he ever encountered compared to this uncertainty, this waiting to see if he and Sarah could work things out. It occupied his heart as well as his head nearly every waking moment.

How many years had he known Sarah? He guessed it

must be over 20; most of their lives. She had always been special. When he'd made a decision for Christ a few years ago, he wasn't long in understanding that any girl he might feel serious about would need to have the same heart for God as he did. There was enough of a change in him that the next time he saw Sarah, she'd eyed him speculatively and asked him what was going on. He didn't immediately answer, for fear of wording things wrong and turning her away forever.

But he need not have worried because the Lord was working in Sarah's heart and she came right to his house to pin him down a few days later.

Ross was surprised speechless when, upon explaining to Sarah about his new life in Christ, her eyes filled with tears and she asked him to pray with her. There was no hesitation then, and Ross walked on a cloud for days.

Neither one saw this as a sign for a future together, but being in each other's company was easier all the time with the newfound faith they both shared. They often came together in excitement to tell some new biblical truth they'd discovered.

In time Ross did take these things to be a sign that this was the wife God had for him. And it seemed Sarah felt the same way, that is until Ross told her of his leading to head out from beneath the protective wings of the man he'd been working for and open up his own practice in Baxter.

"Ross, you can't be serious."

"What do you mean?"

"I mean, why would you want to live all the way down there, where you don't know anyone? You've got a great job with Bill Colter here, and you said he could use you forever."

"I could stay with Bill, Sarah. I know that and I'll never forget what he's taught me, but I want my own practice, small as it might be. And you're wrong about me not knowing anyone in Baxter. Baxter is Paul Cameron's hometown, and I've been to visit with him and Abby. His family is great, the next best thing to being with my own, and in some ways, better."

But she was not convinced and suddenly the future didn't look quite so rosy. The conversation ended when she told him she had never planned to live anywhere other than Hayward.

Shortly after that Ross' plans to move fell quickly into place. Doors opened in ways he never imagined, confirming over and over again that this was God's will and not his own. And still he prayed, begging God to intervene if this was a mistake. With his parent's support he moved to Baxter, taking residence with Grandma Em for an indefinite period.

Now that the question of his moving was out of the way, why hadn't God burdened Sarah's heart with the same destination if they were meant to be together?

Ross knew the answers to his questions were not going to magically appear before his eyes. He had a letter to mail and then work to do. The rest was in God's hands and maybe Sarah's.

15

"Mandy, do you have a minute?"

"Sure."

Amy led the way into her bedroom to the small desk. "Will you please tell me everyone's birthday?"

A few days ago Mandy would have been surprised at such a request, but it didn't take long to learn that Amy was a woman with a generous heart. It made her desire to know everyone's birthday almost routine.

"Start with yourself."

"Okay, I was just 18 on May 9. Carrie will be 15 July 2. Levi is 11 this year on October 27." She paused to let Amy catch up. "Clovis will be 10 in September on the fifteenth. Becca, can you tell Amy your birthday?"

"It's nine something."

"September," her sister supplied.

"Yeah, nine September." Becca spoke from where she'd thrown herself on the bed. Mandy thought as she watched her that Becca acted as if she'd been here forever. She said as much and Amy smiled.

"I hope you all feel that way." There was such sincerity in the words that Mandy knew that now was the time to ask her question.

"Amy, if I was very careful with your books upstairs, I mean, I wouldn't take them out of the room or touch them with dirty hands or anything—well, could I please read some of them?"

Amy looked at Mandy in surprise. Every feeling, every heartwrenching emotion that Mandy had ever felt about books was clearly written on her face. Amy had to fight to keep her voice normal, but she didn't speak soon enough.

"I shouldn't have asked you, Amy. You've already done so much, you must think me the biggest ingrate you've ever known."

"That couldn't be farther from the truth! I think you're one of the sweetest girls I've ever met. I wish you had said something earlier about the books. You could have had one read by now." Mandy watched Amy rise from the desk and move to the door of the wardrobe. When she turned back to Mandy, she held a slim volume bound in black leather.

"Why don't you start with this one? It's a book of poetry that belonged to my mother. It's one of my favorites and I think you'll like it."

"Maybe I better not if it belonged to your mother. Carrie told me about her."

"Take it, Mandy. My mother loved to read, and if she were standing here she'd give it to you herself."

"Thank you," Mandy spoke humbly. "There was one other thing I wanted to ask you."

"Please don't jump on the bed, Becca. Sure, Mandy, what is it?"

"I would like to walk back to my house and get some papers I left behind and leave a note for my pa in case he shows up."

"Oh, what a good idea! I forgot that he'll wonder where you are. I'll tell you what, stay here at my desk and write your note and then when Silas comes back you can take the wagon."

"He's back," Becca chirped as she bounced high in the air.

"Becca, I asked you not to jump on the bed. Now, what did you say?" Amy spoke to the little girl she'd scooped off the bed and now held in her arms.

"Silas is back."

"He is?" She moved to look out the window and sure enough, Silas was coming into the yard.

"Well, don't you have good eyesight! Let's go help unload and give Mandy some quiet to write her note."

Mandy wasn't long at the small desk, and she deliberately said nothing about her mother.

Pa,

    We're staying with Silas and Amy Cameron on the other side of town.

Mandy

Mandy read the note over several times before she folded it and put it into her pocket. Then she joined everyone in the yard.

"Silas, what is all of this?" Mandy heard Amy ask as she approached the wagon. "My list wasn't very long."

"Well, I did some shopping of my own." He had an innocent sparkle in his eye, and Amy wondered how long it would be before she found out what he'd been up to.

"Carrie, what did Mark have to say?"

"He said my throat is better and to keep gargling."

"He doesn't want to see her until next week." Silas supplied the rest of the story as she loaded packages into everyone's arms and told them to take them into the living room.

Amy had just taken some things into the kitchen when he heard Becca squeal with delight in the living room. She went in to find Silas opening package after package of fabric, all lightweight and summery in beautiful blues, greens, yellows, and reds. There were plaids for the boys' shirts and solid colors for special wear, calicos, and even some corduroy. Amy stood in the door and felt tears sting her eyes. Just that morning as she prayed she had asked the Lord to help her broach the subject of clothing to Mandy without offending her.

"*Now,*" Silas was saying, "I didn't know your mother and I wouldn't want to do anything you might consider disrespectful of her memory, but you'll notice I didn't buy any black material. What I'm trying to say is I don't want you to wear black for a year as is sometimes customary. I somehow doubt your mother would have wanted it that way. There is a solid forest green and a navy blue if you feel you really need to be in mourning, but I for one will understand and agree with you if you don't." He had said most of this with his eyes on Mandy and Carrie, for he knew they were the ones who would make this decision. Mandy looked uncertain and Silas steeled himself for whatever she was about to say.

"Everything is wonderful and you're right about Mama, she wouldn't want us to mourn, but Silas, we can't pay for this. Even if I went into town today and found a job, why, it would be months, maybe a year, before I could pay for all of this fabric. I don't mean to put down your hospitality, but we're eating you out of house and home and I think that's enough."

"Mandy," Silas interrupted, for he knew she would go on. "Please listen to what I'm about to say to you. And not just you, Mandy, but all of you. For whatever reason, one that I try not to question, God has not given children to Amy and me. But if He did, I can tell you they would not be paying for their own food and clothing while under my roof. They would have their chores, as I did when I was a kid, and they would help out, the way you all do. However, they would not be working in town or expected to help put food on the table and clothes on our backs.

"If we were struggling financially it might be different, but again for an unknown reason, God has given us more than enough, and we want to share what we have with you.

"The only payment I want is to see the boys in new pants and shirts and you girls in as many dresses and bonnets as this fabric will make. I didn't buy anything for undergarments; I'll leave that up to Amy the next time she's in town." He said all of this comfortingly in his deep, gentle voice. The five children took it all in, on their own individual levels of understanding, and thought he was the most wonderful man on earth.

The first to move or make a sound was Carrie, who came unself-consciously and put her arms around Silas and hugged him. He hugged her back, holding her tight for a moment and kissing her forehead as he released her. Becca needed no prompting after that, for she was clearly the "cuddler" of the group, and Silas gave her a great squeeze before releasing her with a kiss also.

Clovis went for a hug but Silas was sensitive to Levi's feelings, and when the boy held his hand out Silas shook it, even though he wanted to crush the child in his arms. He also ached to hug Mandy, but she stayed across the room from him and thanked him with her heart in her eyes. Silas knew that for now it was enough. She accepted what he said as well as the gift of fabrics, and someday he believed they would be close enough to share an embrace.

He was careful not to look at Amy during any of this, knowing how close to the surface her tears would be. She rescued them both when she said Mandy needed the wagon. They were able to go their separate ways without awkwardness.

16

"Okay, Mandy." Silas lifted her easily onto the wagon seat and handed her the reins. She blinked in surprise, but he didn't notice. "I'll see you when you get back."

When Amy had mentioned taking the wagon, Mandy hadn't really heard the words. If she had, she would have told her immediately that she'd never driven a wagon before. And now as she looked over her shoulder and watched Silas move in his long-legged stride across the yard and back to the house, she wished she'd been more attentive.

"How hard can it be?" She asked the question after a moment's thought and noticed the horse's ears flicked a little. She tried to remember what she'd seen Silas do and almost without realizing it, began imitating him. In the next few seconds she was headed down the road toward town, thankful that the team had been pointed in the right direction.

— ✤ —

Ross sat astride the horse he had borrowed and made mental notes on the land before him. Why would Aaron Marks be interested in this lot? It wasn't very remarkable— Baxter offered much better. From what he could tell after studying the map, it was owned by a man from Reedsburg.

The land to the north was not only owned but occupied. If Ross turned in his saddle he could see the Jackson place, its rundown condition evident from the short distance. Marks had wanted information on that land also. The map showed the Jacksons only owned about six acres. Why would Marks bother? The question nagged his brain as he continued to survey the land.

Vibration on the ground that traveled through the horse and to its rider caused Ross to look for someone approaching. Surprisingly a wagon that looked very much like Silas' came toward the Jackson house at a very brisk pace. The driver sawed on the reins in an abrupt movement that caused the horses to stop but not rest. They tossed their heads and one animal brought his front hooves off the ground.

As Ross heeled his own mount into motion he could easily picture those horses bolting if the holder of those reins did not let up and quickly.

"Ease off on your hold," Ross commanded as he came aside the wild-eyed team. "Easy now." Not until the team was completely settled did he turn to look at who was on the seat.

If he'd thought the horses were frightened and upset, he wasn't sure what to think of Mandy's wide-eyed stare at the animals she obviously had no idea how to handle. Her knuckles were white on the leather straps within her hands, and she didn't seem capable of taking her eyes off the now-calm horses.

"Amanda," Ross called to her from his place by the wagon. His horse stood docile as he'd dismounted and stepped to where he could help her from the seat.

"Amanda." He called to her a second time and reached to take her hands. She let the reins go easily after feeling the pressure of his hands and then stood, still shaken, in front of Ross after he had lowered her to the ground. He watched her cross her arms as though cold and finally knew why he had not been able to dispel her from his thoughts since the day of the funeral. He had never seen a creature in such need of cherishing. He suspected she'd never experienced special treatment or loving care.

"Are you alright?"

"I should have told Silas that I'd never driven a wagon before, but I didn't want him to have to take me. And we were doing fine until a gun went off at the edge of town and the horses nearly broke into a run. I don't think they liked the way I was handling them because they're always calm for Silas. He makes it look so easy." She came to a rather breathless halt and simply looked at Ross. Even though she was a little upset about the horses and wagon, he was a feast for her eyes.

His face was tan and his hat pushed back on his head showed the shine in his hair and the clear blue of his eyes. As Mandy studied him she felt her heart turn over. In the last few days she had convinced herself that he really hadn't been that good-looking and thinking of him had been disrespectful to her Mama. But he was so kind, and Mandy was drawn to him no matter what her head told her heart.

Saying nothing during her scrutiny of him, Ross was still working on the fact that she hadn't told Silas of her inexperience with horses. She could have been seriously hurt. When Silas and Amy found out, he was sure they would be quite upset. And they *would* find out, because when she was finished with whatever business had brought her here, he'd drive her back.

"Thank you for taking care of the horses. I have to go in now and get some things." She turned away and heard him say he'd wait for her.

Mandy didn't argue, even though she felt it unnecessary. She was a little shook but she knew what to do now, at least she thought she did.

There was no sign of her father having been present, but when Mandy stepped through the door she noticed an unfamiliar smell. Assuming the house was musty after being empty, she placed the note on the table and the moved into the bedroom toward the dresser. Mandy reached in the top drawer to a small bundle of papers held together by an old string. She wasn't sure what all would be in the sheaf but she wanted to wait until she was back in her room at Camerons to open it.

Closing the drawer, Mandy stopped as the corner of an old photograph caught her eye. She lifted it carefully from beneath an old shirt of her father's and stared in awe.

"Amanda?" When she didn't answer his summons from the kitchen Ross stepped to the door of the bedroom to find her. She didn't look up from the photo, and Ross moved behind her to see what held her attention. He sucked in a quick breath when he saw the image on the paper. It was Amanda, a beautiful Amanda.

"It's my mother." Mandy spoke as though she could read his thoughts. "I've never seen it before. I can't think why she never had it out."

The woman in the picture was not the woman that Mandy knew, recognizable, but not the way she remembered, and Mandy was fascinated by what she saw. The woman in the picture did not have deep lines of disappointment, hard work, and grief etched on her face. Her cheeks were not sunken and loose. The children had never seen this face, a face that radiated happiness and peace with no worries of where the next meal would come from, or how cold the next winter would be and whether the wood box would hold.

Mandy hugged the picture to her for just a moment before making her way back out to the wagon. As she walked, her mind conjured up a fleeting memory of the young woman in the picture smiling at her.

Ross was right behind Mandy, and she saw instantly that he'd turned the team around and tied his own mount to the back.

"You really don't have to ride with me, Ross, although I thank you for your trouble."

"You could have been hurt if this team had run away with you. Your family needs you right now, and I *will* see you back to Silas' to make sure you get there unhurt and in one piece." Ross immediately regretted his tone with her.

He watched Mandy take a step away from him and eye

him warily, her papers and photo clasped to her as though they could offer some sort of protection.

Ross realized then that he had never experienced anything like this before. There were no games in her, no pretense. The girls back home would have said such a thing just so he would insist, knowing all along that the gentleman in him wouldn't let them go alone. But Amanda Jackson put on no act. She honestly believed she could get herself home and didn't want to trouble him.

She didn't say anything or offer any resistance when he helped her into the wagon, but her body was very stiff and she sat like a statue on the seat beside him. Ross was at a total loss for words at the moment, thinking anything he might say would only make matters worse. So he moved the team forward with a prayer in his heart that he hadn't just scared this girl away forever. Why that was so important to him, he was not in the mood to analyze.

17

They rode all the way through town before Mandy broke the silence. Ross would have been surprised to know that she wasn't pouting or upset with the way he'd spoken to her. In fact he probably would have chosen for her to be upset rather than so accepting of the way he'd talked to her.

"I wasn't sure if I'd see you again, Ross, but after my mother's funeral I realized I reached over and held your hand during the service, and I wanted to thank you for not slapping my hand away or anything when we were all having such a hard day."

He wondered if she would ever stop surprising him. "You're not upset with me then?"

"No, of course not; I just thanked you. It was a very kind thing for you to do. After all, we hadn't even met yet."

"No, I'm not talking about your hand at the funeral, although if it was a comfort I'm glad. I'm talking about at your house today."

It took Mandy a moment to answer. "I'm not upset that you saw my mother's picture. What made you think that?"

Ross brought the wagon to a complete halt in the road outside of town. She really didn't know. He looked at the face so close to his shoulder and saw nothing but curiosity.

"Are you okay, Ross? Oh," she blushed suddenly. "Maybe I shouldn't call you Ross. I figured us to be the same age and you were introduced as Ross but maybe I'm out of line."

For the first time in Ross didn't know how many years, he wanted to cry. "Amanda," he spoke in an almost hoarse voice, "I'm glad you call me Ross and we are, I think, about the same age. But I thought you were upset with me because of how high-handed I was about driving the wagon home." Ross desperately wished he'd kept his mouth shut.

"I don't know what you mean."

"In that case it's not important, as long as I didn't upset you."

"No, I'm fine. It's not as if you hit me or called me a name or anything personal. People are more important than wagons, and if you feel better driving then that's fine." She was so matter-of-fact about it all that once again words deserted Ross and he moved the wagon on.

When they were in the yard a few minutes later, Ross stayed in his seat and helped Mandy to the ground with one hand. She thanked him with a smile and a few words that he barely heard and went toward the house as if she didn't have a care in the world.

Ross slapped the reins once more and moved the wagon up to the barn. Stepping down, he hoped to find Silas inside.

"Well, Ross!" Luke spoke with surprise as both he and Silas approached. "What brings you out this way?"

"I need to talk with you, Silas." Ross was very obviously upset.

"Why don't you boys go out and swing? And take turns," Luke called after the swiftly retreating backs of Levi, Clovis, and his own Josh. "Should I make myself scarce?"

"No, Luke, I don't think that's necessary. It's just that I was surveying some land out by the Jackson place when Amanda drove up. She'd never driven a wagon before today but didn't want to trouble Silas with having to take her, so she decided not to mention it."

"Oh no! Is she okay?" Silas' entire body had tensed and Ross was quick to assure him.

"She's fine. But the horses were just short of being out of control after a shot was fired near town. She nearly split their mouths open when she stopped them. It was God alone, I'm sure, that kept them from bolting and taking Amanda on the ride of her life.

"But that's not all I'm upset about—it's Amanda herself. I've never known a girl with so little fight in her. I told her that I would drive the wagon back, and because she'd scared me I wasn't very nice about it. She's completely accepting of any order given to her, and this thing today tells me it never even occurs to her to ask for help.

"Maybe you think I'm overreacting, but she scares me. We can't assume anything where she is concerned, and I just thought with her beneath your roof, Silas, you'd want to know."

Silas was shaken. "You're sure she's okay?"

"I'm sure."

"It never even occurred to me that she wouldn't know how to handle a team. There's so little about her, *all of them*, that I know. The little ones are easy, but Mandy, and Carrie too, to some degree, are a little out of my range. They can't be treated like children, and handling them gently is tougher.

"And Ross, I don't think you're overreacting. Amy has cried at some point every day that they've been with us. The worst time is at meals when they look at the food as if they're afraid it's going to disappear right off the table. Mandy always looks to make sure the other kids have food on their plates before she eats her own. I know she'd go without for them and probably has many times.

"Did you know that they thought no one would be at the funeral? They said they didn't get out much and that we shouldn't go to the trouble to plan food for so many." Tears gathered in the big man's eyes, and he did nothing to hide them.

"I've never gone without food a day in my life. You should have seen the looks on their faces when they found out we have three meals a day, *every* day." A tear spilled over then, and Luke reached for his own handkerchief.

The men stood in silence then, each collecting himself. Silas had just thanked Ross for coming and telling him about Mandy when a loud scream split the air.

18

"Get it out of here, Levi!" Mandy ordered her brother in a furious voice. "Can't you see you're scaring everyone to death?"

"Well, that's dumb. There's nothing to be scared about. He's just a baby."

Levi held the snake in his hands a little bit higher and examined it with pride. Clovis looked at Amy in something akin to awe; he'd never heard a sound quite like that scream before. He almost hoped she'd do it again, but not because she was scared. He didn't want her to be upset as she obviously was now.

"We better go out, Lee."

"No, I want to take Henry to my room."

"No!" The word came from Amy, Mandy, and Carrie in unison just as the men hit the back door at a full run. They stood just inside and took in the scene in silence.

Amy and Carrie were both behind the kitchen table as far as they could get from the three little boys and their newfound pet. Mandy looked like an enraged warrior in front of them with a look that clearly said she'd had enough.

Levi looked thoroughly offended that no one was the least bit proud of the great catch he'd found in the yard. Clovis, always at Levi's side, was taking it in stride while five-year-old Joshua looked as if Levi and Clovis were the answers to all his prayers.

Silas' hand went up to rub at his mustache in a manner familiar to both Luke and Amy.

"Silas!" Amy's voice was outraged that he was actually thinking of laughing at this horrible situation. She wondered if her heart would ever beat normally again. She looked over at Luke and Ross, but they had both taken a great interest in the floor. Amy told herself she would never forgive them.

"I'll say it one more time, Levi. Get that snake out of here!"

"No! Silas make her listen to me. It's just a little one and I want to keep it in my room." This little announcement momentarily sobered Silas faster than anything else could have, and he shook his head no.

"Take it outside, Levi." There was no argument this time and the boys filed out—the fun was over.

Silas did not immediately go to his wife, but he watched her with the laughter back in his eyes.

"I can't believe you're laughing about this." Her outraged, flushed face was too much for the men and their laughter shook the room. Luke dropped heavily into a chair and Ross leaned against the wall. Silas made an attempt at sobering, but each time he looked at Amy he dissolved again into laughter. He knew he was going to be in big trouble for this, but he couldn't seem to contain himself.

By the time Amy and Carrie came out from behind the table, Mandy was seeing the humor herself. Her eyes met Carrie's and they both smiled. Amy didn't miss the look and said, "I can see I'm hopelessly outnumbered."

Silas went to her then and pulled her into his arms. "You looked so cute, sweetheart. I thought your eyes were going to come right out of your head."

She tried to look angry but couldn't muster a glare. She gave Silas a soft punch and he released her. He went to Carrie next and offered her a hug after which she smiled at him good-naturedly. It seemed the most natural thing in the world to go to Mandy next and hug her. To his surprise she was receptive to his embrace and smiled when he praised her.

"Mandy, I'm very impressed. You stood right up to Levi, snake and all. I'm also glad Becca is with Christine and Kate."

"That makes two of us and Silas is right Mandy, you were very brave."

"For all the good it did me. Levi was determined to have Henry in his room."

"I had a snake named Henry." Ross' voice was so matter-of-fact that the laughter was rekindled.

"Where did they find it?" Silas finally asked Amy. She said she didn't know and she didn't care but she wanted it out of the yard and far away from her garden before she went out to water later.

Silas said he would see to it. The men, still chuckling, took their leave to check on the boys and get back to their jobs.

19

Sunday morning Amy lay against Silas in her usual pre-rising fashion, marveling that Mandy, Carrie, Levi, Clovis, and Becca had been with them for an entire week. Already there was such a change in them. They looked different certainly, more filled out and healthier, but the biggest change was in their attitudes. Each of them save Mandy, who was coming along at her own pace, roamed all over the house as though it was his own, and in Amy's mind it was.

Christine had asked her outright how she coped. Amy, in all honesty, had not understood the question. Things weren't picked up all the time like they used to be, and the floors needed sweeping almost constantly. But then there never used to be little hugs from small people who just waited for your embrace and hugged you back, nor little faces at the supper table shining with delight when you brought in a chocolate cake, nor little boys running in the back door to tell you of the horses they rode. Experiences Amy wouldn't trade for all the quiet or clean floors in the world.

Not that it was all fun. Amy fell into bed every night in a state of exhaustion. And there were scenes—like the one at the supper table the night before with Becca—

"I don't like green beans."

"You don't have too many. Please eat them, Becca."

"No! I won't, Amy, and you can't make me!" After which she threw herself to the floor in the dining room and had a screaming fit. Stunned, Amy didn't move. Rising from his chair without a word, Silas picked up the crying five-year-old and put her on her feet. The flat of his hand connected one time, very hard, on the backside of her dress before she was placed back in her chair.

"When Amy tells you to eat your green beans, you eat your beans, Becca." She did, without further protest. Amy thanked Silas later for handling it. He told her how much he'd hated to spank Becca, but they both agreed it would be easier for everyone if the children knew what was expected of them and did it without complaint.

And the episode with the wagon, which had been frightening. "You should have told us, Mandy," Silas had said later.

"Ross told you all about it?"

"Yes."

"Well, it wasn't so bad and I really didn't want you to have to take me."

"It would have been no trouble, Mandy, and I hate to think what might have happened to you. Next time you need something, just ask. If I don't have time I'll tell you. And stop thinking of yourself as trouble. We don't feel that way."

Mandy had nodded and smiled, but Silas and Amy were not sure if she really believed them.

And then there had been the snake. Amy felt a shiver go through her at the thought. It was an episode from which she was certain she would never recover.

"Are you cold?" Silas gently slid his arms around her.

"No I was just thinking of the snake."

He immediately began to chuckle, causing Amy to become indignant. She tried to move away from him, but he would have none of it. It had become a wrestling match before Silas stopped laughing and Amy stopped fighting him.

"Are you mad?"

"Yes," and she was, a little.

"I'll try not to laugh anymore." His voice was still highly amused and Amy was dubious. "By the way, I'm not the only one who gets into trouble with his wife. Luke told me he teased Christine the other day and made her cry."

"I hope he spent the day in the doghouse," Amy instantly sided with her sister-in-law. "The last thing Christine needs in her condition is teasing. And Luke has a way of doing it with such a straight face that it's hard to know if he really *is* teasing."

They lay quietly for a moment. Then above them they heard the sound of feet hitting the floor.

"We better get up if we're going to be to church on time."

"You're right. I'll put the coffee on and then get the boys going before I head to the barn. And Amy, I'm sorry I laughed. Really." He punctuated his apology with a kiss.

"And I forgive you. Really."

— ✣ —

"You can wait until the service is over." Silas whispered the words to Levi who asked, for the third time, if he could be excused. "Next time, go before the service starts."

Silas, as a boy, would have vowed never to inflict such misery on his own children but as he looked back, he knew that the only thing that ever taught him to see to his personal needs ahead of the service was having to sit through a few sermons in agony.

Silas and Amy were not in the miserable condition that Levi was in, but neither were they getting much out of this service. The first one in the pew had been Mandy, then Becca, then Carrie. Silas felt it a good idea to put Becca between her sisters, hoping she would stay quiet. Next to Carrie was Amy and then Clovis, Silas, and Levi on the end. Anyway, that was the way it started out.

Silas lost track of how many times Becca had gotten up to come down and get her nose wiped. Finally Amy had given her the handkerchief, but she lost it within three minutes so Silas took her on his lap, which miraculously stopped her running nose.

Between Levi's having to go outside, Becca's running nose, and Clovis' feet and legs that would not keep still, Silas felt like the pew hosted "The Cameron Family Side Show." Maybe it was the heat, Silas thought, as he watched a stern-faced Mark take both Emily and Eliza out, who at nearly ten and six, were both old enough to sit through the service.

Suddenly he envisioned Sunday dinner at Grandma Em's with all 24 of them, 11 adults and 13 kids, and wasn't sure he was up to it.

— ✢ —

"Now, I think we're all set." Grandma Em said the words with a smile and took her place in the dining room. "Silas would you give thanks today?"

He stood and moved from his place at the table to the doorway between the kitchen and dining room to see if everyone in both rooms was quiet for prayer. He thanked God for the five additions to the family and the one on the way. He asked God's blessing on the food and the hands that prepared it and then took his seat back in the kitchen.

They had, for the fun of it that day, set the tables for all the boys in the kitchen and the girls in the dining room.

Sue had her hands full with all four of her girls at the table. Mandy and Carrie impressed everyone in the dining room by assisting Ellen and Erika throughout the meal.

What everyone wasn't to know was how grateful Mandy was to have a little girl to take care of. Children she could handle; she'd been doing so all of her life. But conversation with adults, even though she knew she was considered one herself, was usually awkward and embarrassing. It was a relief for Mandy that nearly everyone at the table was busy with a little person, sparing her from making conversation.

The meal didn't take long and Julia, Amy, Mandy, and Carrie cleaned up and did the dishes in record time. The day was warm and everyone had moved out of doors to the front porch and yard. The cleanup crew made their way outside when the work was done. They had just settled onto the porch when a verbal fight broke out among Levi, Clovis, and Charlie at the corner of the house.

Faster than anyone anticipated, it moved from verbal to physical and within seconds the three were rolling on the ground. Surprise held almost everyone immobile, which gave Carrie and Mandy, who were beyond surprise, a chance to move off the porch and wade into the flailing arms and legs as though they did so everyday.

Carrie laid hold of Clovis and Mandy easily handled Levi. Charlie picked himself up and would have come forward again but saw that his opponents were being firmly held. Mac was next to arrive on the scene, and he looked furious with Charlie. Silas was on Mac's heels and immediately said he wanted an explanation.

"I said I expect an explanation and I mean right now!" He repeated himself when the boys stood reticent.

"Charlie, you go first," his father ordered.

"He said you drank."

"He said I *what*?" asked a totally confused Mac.

"Levi said all men drink and I said my dad didn't."

"That isn't all you said." Clovis spoke with uncharacteristic anger, and the three fell silent again.

"What else did you say, Charlie?" Appearing embarrassed and reluctant, the boy didn't answer. Mac took hold of his arm, but he still said nothing.

"He said our pa is a drunk and he's not!" Levi's eyes were filled with tears as he said the words.

"Charles, you will apologize right now." The command itself told Charlie his father would brook no disobedience.

"I'm sorry I said that about your pa." It was obvious he meant it by the look of regret on his face.

"Now, Clovis, Levi, you apologize. Mac doesn't drink and you know very well I don't drink, so you were wrong, too."

There were apologies and small nods all around and then Charlie took himself off to where the other adults were keeping the rest of the children from interfering.

When Levi spoke only Silas, Clovis, Mandy, and Carrie were within earshot. "Don't think I don't know he's a drunk." His eyes were still filled with tears and he faced Silas defiantly. "But he's still my pa and I'll knock anyone down who dares to bad-mouth him to my face. Come on, Clovis."

Silas felt defeat wash over him as the two little boys retreated to the backyard alone.

"He doesn't deserve that kind of loyalty." Mandy spoke as she too watched her brothers leave. "He's never been a good pa, but like Levi said, he *is* our pa." Both girls moved then to follow the boys. Silas watched them go, praying with all of his heart—for what, he was not sure.

20

Ross looked up from his desk as the door opened. He smiled and leaned back in his chair at the sight of Peter Culver, his future housemate, leaning against the closed door.

"Well, Pete, what brings you out of that fancy office at the bank?" Ross posed the question to the good-natured man.

Pete worked at the bank and had an office with a window. The fact that the bank building was owned by Pete's uncle had something to do with this. That wasn't to insinuate that Pete had not worked for the privilege. More than one person had been fooled, by his relaxed attitude toward life, into thinking he was a bit slow-witted. Ross knew firsthand that this was not the case.

"I was at the post office and you had a letter, so I just thought I'd bring it by."

"Thanks." Ross took the letter from the outstretched hand and felt his heart quicken upon recognizing Sarah's handwriting. *She must have mailed this the very day I left*, he thought and wondered what it would say.

"Bad news?"

"I don't know," Ross answered honestly.

"Well, if it's Sarah telling you to go fly a kite, the girls in Baxter will be rejoicing."

"You don't know what you're talking about."

"That's where you're wrong, my friend. You didn't notice the girls who turned in their seats on Sunday as you came up the aisle."

"I do not go to church to turn the heads of the young ladies."

"No, I guess you don't. As a matter of fact, neither do I. But when a guy is having a nice little chat before the service with the very attractive Candy Hunter, and then this guy's friend walks in and suddenly Candy forgets he's even there, well, let's just say it's a bit discouraging."

"I didn't even see Candy yesterday."

"That's my point. From what I could see, the only girl you saw was Mandy Jackson."

"Mandy Jackson?"

"Hey, Ross, take it easy. I'm not criticizing your choice. She's real easy on the eyes."

"Don't you talk about her like that!" Ross was instantly on the defensive.

"Oh, so that's the way the wind blows," Pete said with a knowing smile.

"No, it's not. It's just that the Jacksons have had a real hard time of it lately, and I don't like that kind of talk where Amanda is concerned."

Peter eyed Ross for a moment and then shrugged. "You're right. It is a rather flip way to refer to a lovely lady like Mandy Jackson. But I better warn you—if you're feeling something for her, you'd better speak up. Every guy in church yesterday had his eye on her."

"All six of them, you mean?" Ross' voice was unconcerned.

"It only takes one." Pete turned away after making that remark and didn't see the thoughtful look on Ross' face.

"Well, I'm back to work. Oh, I almost forgot to tell you, my uncle said the house would be ready next week."

"Next week! That's great."

"Yeah, I think so too. I'll talk to you later."

— ✥ —

"Ross! You're home for lunch. What's the occasion?"

"No occasion really. I need to read a letter from Sarah without worrying that someone will come into the office."

Grandma Em looked compassionate and Ross sat down on the nearest chair in the kitchen. "She couldn't have received the letter I just sent, so it makes me wonder what she has to say. Something tells me it's not good news."

"I'm sorry, Ross."

"Thanks, but I'm not sure if I'm sorry or not. I guess I'm just too much of a romantic. I always pictured that love would come for me as it did for my mother. She said that she was walking down the street when she saw a small boy run into the road. Without even looking she charged into the street and then froze, putting herself and the child both in danger of being run over by a fast-approaching wagon. My father witnessed the whole thing from a few yards away and rushed after them.

"She said when they'd arrived safely on the walk and the boy skipped away unhurt, she looked up to find my father's arms still around her. She said it was love at first sight. He came calling that night, and they were engaged and married five weeks later. My father always jokes that it would have been a lot sooner but my mother insisted on a church wedding—fancy dress and all.

"The first time I saw your granddaughter-in-law, Abby, I was sure it had happened to me just like mother said. But she ended up being the answer to my spiritual needs and believe me, I'm not complaining." Grandma Em nodded, remembering Ross telling her about this not long after he moved in.

"Now with Sarah, it wasn't love at first sight because we'd known each other so long. It was more like a feeling of rightness. That, along with our bond in the Lord, and of course we care for each other. And well we just sort of—"

"But there's no real spark."

"No. No spark." He looked as if the thought had just occurred to him. Then he rose. "I'll be in my room for a while. If I have time later I'll grab a bite to eat."

Grandma Em sat for a time where he'd left her. The yearning for the companionship she'd had with Joseph had never completely abated but at least the unsureness of youth was gone. They'd had many wonderful years together and now he was with the Lord. And someday she would be too.

But how many times had she been through this with her own son and grandchildren? She wasn't sure what the exact count was, but all of them had followed a pattern that somehow led up to the good marriages they all shared.

First came their faith in the Lord. Not even Luke, who met Christine before she was saved, ever entertained thoughts of marrying a non-Christian.

She was sure that each one had experienced some sort of misery in the waiting game. It was the spark that she and Ross spoke briefly of, which caused that. If they hadn't wanted desperately to be together, there would have been no tension about the future.

It was easier, she was convinced, to make a decision about your life mate if you had God to turn to. But it didn't change the uncertainty of the moment, the yearnings and the needs. Grandma Em knew Ross to be in this state and her keen memory of her own life and the lives of others within her reach caused her to be able to pray with great compassion.

— ✥ —

Dear Ross,

It's hard that you're leaving tomorrow morning and there are things between us that are unsettled. It's not the same, but I'll try to say to you in this letter the things I was not able to say in person.

I don't believe that any of this is your fault. You are acting as you feel God leads, and that is how it should be. But I can't help but wonder about myself. I mean, wouldn't a woman who loved a man be willing to go anywhere he is, just to be with him? Maybe our friendship has been too close, but something is wrong with the way I feel and I don't think either one of us should force this.

What I mean by that is—I want you to consider yourself free to see other girls. I will consider myself free in the same way, but please don't think I'm out looking—I'm not.

I know this hurts you. I hurt, too. But right now, and I think you would agree, I can't see us as husband and wife.

Please write back to me Ross. Please stay in touch so I know how you're feeling. I think I'll always love you. I'm just not *in* love with you. Does that make sense? Write when you get this. I'll wait to hear from you.

Love, Sarah

— ✤ —

"It makes perfect sense," Ross said to the empty room. There was something wrong with the fact that she was not willing to follow him anywhere. There was also something wrong with the fact that he was more relieved than upset at knowing there was probably no future for them.

Ross read the letter once again and was again surprised to find himself so relieved. He'd write back to Sarah immediately and thank her for her wisdom. Unbidden, Peter's words came back to him. "The only girl you saw was Mandy Jackson."

Ross shook his head. Pete had only misinterpreted his glancing her way to see how the whole family was getting along. An image came to mind of Amanda on the wagon seat, the reins clenched in her hands. Then in front of the dresser holding her mother's picture and finally, thanking him for not slapping her hand away when she'd reached for him at the funeral.

Ross was convinced at that moment that the most dangerous thing on earth was a slim, hazel-eyed woman who'd never known a day of comfort in her life. *Stay away from her, Ross, no matter what Pete says. Stay away from her.*

21

"Leave me alone!" Rebecca screamed the words at Amy. Amy watched in confusion as Becca tried to push the sofa with her small body and hide behind it.

"Becca, honey, what is it?" Amy implored the child from a nonthreatening distance, but Becca continued to sob and tried to make herself as small as possible against the living room wall.

"What happened?" The question came from Mandy, who had heard the noise from upstairs.

"I honestly don't know. Becca fell asleep on the sofa during the story I was telling her and when I tried to put a blanket over her, she woke up and began to scream. All I can think of is that I must have startled her." Amy described the scene to the accompaniment of Becca's cries.

Mandy pulled her youngest sister away from the wall and into her arms. Becca struggled, kicking and screaming, but Mandy held fast. And after what seemed an eternity, the little girl collapsed in her arms. In a pitiful and nearly indistinguishable voice, Becca said, "I want Mama."

Amy sank into a nearby chair and did nothing to hide her tears. The grief had to come, she knew that. These children had adjusted so quickly to the move, but their mother still lived in their hearts, just as she should, and their pain was still very real. Amy, however, hadn't been prepared for such a violent reaction. She didn't take it personally. Becca had probably been dreaming and hadn't recognized where she was when Amy woke her.

The cries were quieting now, with only an occasional call for her mother. Mandy continued to hold her and scrutinize Amy.

"Are you alright?"

"I think so," Amy answered quietly.

"Carrie told me that Becca cried in the night for Mama. Did she tell you?"

Amy shook her head no.

"I know that Becca likes you. Silas too. But I think coming here so soon after Mama's death sort of crowded out some of the grief in our minds. Now the newness is wearing off. It's becoming routine to have enough to eat and a soft bed to sleep in. But with the wonder of it wearing off, we have more time to think. And naturally our thoughts turn to Mama and Pa."

Amy was struck momentarily dumb by Mandy's speech and then, "Mandy," she said softly, "I think you're wonderful."

"You do?" She was genuinely surprised.

"Yes, I do! I knew you would all begin to miss your mother, but I never thought of it in regard to your moving here and well, you just explained it all so logically, I just—"

Amy seemed to run out of words and Mandy smiled at her. "I think you're pretty nice, too."

Amy joined her on the sofa then and held her hands out for Rebecca. The little girl did not hesitate to crawl into Amy's lap, and she held her close. Mandy watched them, thinking that Amy was the most giving and forgiving person she'd ever met.

"Amy, will you promise me something?" Mandy spoke in a whisper and marveled that she was actually going to ask this.

"If I can, Mandy."

"Will you please promise to be my friend, even when Pa comes back and takes us away?"

"Oh, Mandy, you can't believe what an easy promise that is to make." Emotion choked Amy and she barely forced the words out.

Mandy shifted until her head was near Amy's shoulder, and Amy moved around until all three of them were touching and resting close together on the sofa.

Becca squirmed some and Mandy said, "Amy, why did you and Silas take us in?" Mandy heard Amy sigh, and it was a few moments before she spoke.

"I sometimes have a hard time accepting God's will that Silas and I have not had children of our own. The Sunday morning you came to live with us I knew another month had come and I was not pregnant. And I wanted to be pregnant so badly—I can't tell you how badly."

Mandy heard the rough sincerity in her voice and shifted so she could watch her face. Becca became restless at that moment and with the resilience of a child, hopped to the floor and moved to the corner of the living room where Amy kept her old doll and cradle.

"Silas and I had words that morning because I was so upset and we were very late for church. But at the end of the service, which was about all we'd made it for, Uncle Chad asked for prayer for the Jackson family and shared that your mother had died. I can't explain it, Mandy. It was as if God's hand reached down and touched me, and I knew that I wanted you all to come here to our home and live for as long as you needed.

"We had lunch with Uncle Chad and Aunt April that afternoon, and we discussed it with them. I think you know the rest." Mandy was looking so surprised that Amy questioned her.

"Mandy, what is it?"

"What you said about God reaching down and touching you. I think the same thing happened to me when Pastor Chad and Silas came to the house. I just knew we *had* to go with them."

"That doesn't surprise me, Mandy. I feel God has had His hand in all of our lives from the first day."

"I didn't agree with what Pastor Chad said on Sunday," Mandy said suddenly, and almost fiercely.

"About what exactly?" Amy hadn't heard a word of the sermon.

"About everyone sinning and needing a Savior. I believe in God, Amy, but I don't think people sin. I mean, everyone makes mistakes, but that's not sin. We're here to work hard with the bodies He gives us and at the end of our years we die, but it's not hopeless. If you were a good person and did your best, then life goes on for those after us."

"Mandy, I respect your belief, but I want you to know that I disagree. The Bible says "all sin," and I can tell you in my own life that it's very true."

"I don't believe that, Amy. You never sin."

"Yes, Mandy, I do. I was born a sinner. And that causes me to have a need for a Savior. I believe that Savior to be Jesus Christ."

"Jesus, of the Bible?"

"Yes. God's Son. Sent to earth for that very purpose—to die on the cross for sins." Amy had said all of this with gentle surety and Mandy was all ears.

"So you believe in hell?"

"The Bible says it's there."

"You believe everything the Bible says?"

"Mandy, please don't think it's easy or that I always live as I should, but yes, I believe the Bible to be the Word of God. And the most wonderful thing in the Word of God is that Christ died for us. But that's not all. The Bible says that when we trust in Him, He lives within us and helps us to trust and obey Him." Amy watched her face to see how she was taking in the words, but Mandy gave nothing away.

Just then the wagon and horses sounded in the yard with Silas, Carrie, and the boys. "I think everyone is back so we're about to be interrupted. Mandy, will you think on all I've said?"

"Sure." Mandy's reply was quiet, her face thoughtful. "Can we talk more later?"

"We most certainly can," Amy replied as her heart took wing.

22

"Hello, Mr. Marks. What can I do for you?"

"I want to know what you found out with the maps in town." The voice was gruff, with no hint of a question or request, a voice used to issuing commands, not asking questions.

Ross had been sure this was the reason he'd been summoned to Aaron Marks' office, but he wanted to be certain.

"Well, I think it's pretty much what you expected it to be. Why did you want to know?"

"That's none of your business."

"I think it is. For instance, if you were interested in farming, I could recommend the best acres to buy. Are you interested in farming?"

"No!"

"Well, that's good because it's very rocky out there and I would say not very fertile. Of course I'm no expert—"

"Just tell me what you found out! Whose name is on the plat map and what's it worth!"

Ross eyed the man for a long moment. He'd deliberately baited him, and though he was growing agitated Aaron Marks showed no signs of giving anything away.

"Except for the few acres owned by Ward Jackson, the land is owned by a man named Brooks. His address is Reedsburg."

"And the cost of everything?"

"Beyond finding out that none of the land is for sale, I did no inquiring. The value being in that case, irrelevant."

He saw the older man's face suffuse with color and knew he had overstepped his bounds. Ross could see that Aaron Marks was barely holding his temper. A boy came in just then and laid some mail on the desk. Drawing his glance down, Ross saw a familiar name on a piece of stationery.

L.C. Brooks
Reedsburg, Wisconsin

"Did you think you were the only shark I had working for me?" Marks had followed the line of Ross' gaze. "I'm a businessman, Beckett, and a businessman always covers his tracks." He obviously took great relish in telling Ross this, assuming it would crush the spirit of this impertinent young lawyer. He'd let him dangle for a while and then when the kid begged a little, he'd find some petty job for him. He might prove to be useful for some future projects.

But Aaron Marks didn't know there were people in the world like Ross Beckett—people who did not have a price.

"Well, Mr. Marks, I'll assume then that you'll no longer be needing my services. I'll drop my bill in the mail."

Aaron Marks' jaw nearly swung on its hinges as Ross' broad-shouldered frame swung out the door and onto the street. Ross, on the other hand, moved toward his own office with a light step.

"What a relief," he thought. "Everything that man does makes me uneasy." They wouldn't be working together again, Ross was certain, and even as it gave him a keen feeling of respite, he knew he would be keeping a subtle eye on the future dealings of Aaron Marks.

23

"I think they're finally settled. I sure hope the girls don't catch this."

"Or you," Silas said as he lovingly brushed the hair off Amy's forehead. Amy was just coming to bed at 4:30 A.M. Both Clovis and Levi had had the stomach flu through the evening and on into the night. Silas and Amy had gone to bed around midnight. Amy, as usual, did not fall right to sleep, so she was the one to hear Clovis up again. She went to him without waking Silas.

The action had been pretty nonstop after that. Amy had moved Levi to the living room because he needed to make continual trips to the privy; Amy was glad it was a warm night.

The flu affected Clovis in the opposite way, and Amy kept a pail near his bed. She explained all of this to Silas as she fell into bed. He had not even realized she'd been up after midnight.

"You've been up all night?" Silas asked, wondering how he'd slept through the noise.

"I think so."

"Amy," he chided her. "You should have called me. What time is it?"

"I don't know," she answered on a yawn.

Silas told her he'd make sure the boys were better before he left in the morning and then he would take the girls to church and let her and the boys sleep. Amy answered him, but she was so tired he only hoped she'd understood.

"I feel bad about Amy being up with the boys." Mandy spoke from her seat in the wagon as she, Carrie, Becca, and Silas headed toward town. They'd left the house early, before breakfast. Silas said he wanted the house to be quiet for Amy and the boys, so they were headed to Grandma Em's to eat.

"She and the boys are sleeping now. We're going home right after church, so they won't be alone for too long."

"Are you sure we should drop in on your grandma, Silas? Maybe she doesn't have enough breakfast for all of us."

"Believe me, Mandy, she'll love it."

And she did, even though she was concerned about the boys and Amy. There was already plenty of coffee on the stove, and Grandma Em made up a big pot of cereal. Eggs, fresh apple muffins, and juice were added and by the time everyone pushed their plates away they were more than satisfied.

As was her morning routine, Grandma Em reached for her Bible, and turned the pages for a few moments. She passed her Bible to Silas when she was satisfied with the passage she had found.

"Will you please read, Si—the ones I have underlined."

"It would be my pleasure. Philippians 4:1-13, 'Therefore, my brethren dearly beloved and longed for, my joy and crown, so stand fast in the Lord, dearly beloved. I beseech Euodia, and beseech Syntyche, that they be of the same mind in the Lord. And I entreat thee also, true yokefellow, help those women who labored with me in the gospel, with Clement also, and with other my fellowlabourers, whose names are in the book of life.'"

"What is the book of life?" Carrie asked, as soon as Silas was done speaking.

"The book of life is where your name is written when you believe that you've sinned and that Jesus Christ died for your sins," Silas answered her.

"Amy and I talked about Jesus Christ a few days ago, but I still can't believe that God thinks we sin." Silas was not surprised by Mandy's words because Amy had told him of their conversation. Silas knew exactly what he would say to her if he had the chance, but his grandmother spoke first.

"I used to feel that way, Mandy, that there must be something I could do that was good enough to get me to heaven. I obeyed my parents and usually did the things I knew to be right, honestly believing I didn't sin. But then one day my mother read to me from the chapter before the one Silas read. Silas, read in chapter 3, verse 4."

"'Though I might also have confidence in the flesh. If any other man thinketh that he hath reasons for which he might trust in the flesh, I more.'"

"Now, Mandy," Grandma Em went on. "The apostle Paul wrote this and he had done many things on his own, 'in the flesh' is how he put it, trying to win God's approval. The next verses in chapter three tell some of the things he did. In fact, he did so many *good* things that he was willing to challenge anyone who thought they'd done more. But he goes on to say in verse 9, that it all means nothing, that without Jesus Christ, the things Paul did count for nothing in eternity. Silas, please read that verse."

"'And be found in him, not having mine own righteousness, which is of the Law, but that which is through the faith of Christ, the righteousness which is of God by faith.'"

"We don't have to be a murderer to be called a sinner. Next to God's holiness we are *so* imperfect. We can't possibly do anything good enough to be called a Christian and go to heaven some day. But the wonderful part of it is that we don't *have* to do anything. Jesus Christ did it all, and we just need to admit our sin and believe in Him. He does the rest."

Carrie and Mandy exchanged a look. "Mama believed that. Her pa was a preacher. She tried to explain it to us one time but Levi got mad and said if God was so good why did we go hungry and cold? Mama didn't say too much after that, but I know she prayed for us."

Silas and Grandma Em were both surprised at this new insight into the children. Grandma Em asked, "Did you children ever know your grandfather, the one who was a preacher?"

"No," Mandy answered. "Mama never talked much about her parents or where she grew up. I can't think why she never showed us that photograph of her; it's so pretty."

Grandma Em looked to Silas in question. "When Mandy went back to her house to get some papers, she found an old daguerreotype of her mother and brought it back to the house."

"It's in my room and I look at every night before I go to bed."

"Has it been a comfort to have her picture and papers, Mandy?" Grandma Em asked gently.

"The picture, yes, but the papers, well, I haven't looked at them yet. Somehow reading them seems like the most final act. I mean, no matter what I read, no matter what the papers say, I can't ask her any questions. I have no way of finding out what anything may have meant. And I'm also realizing what a private person Mama was. Looking at the papers somehow feels like I'm intruding into a part of her she wanted left private."

The adults at the table nodded with understanding. They could see it was time to close the conversation. The dishes had to be left or they would be late to church.

24

Silas walked into church with his three girls and Grandma Em and immediately noticed Aunt April sitting alone in a front pew. He directed the girls her way.

The first one in the pew was Carrie, so she ended up next to the pastor's wife. Silas sat next to Carrie with Becca in his lap and Grandma Em and Mandy on his other side.

Silas had to speak to Becca only twice about squirming. Other than his mind taking occasional trips home to Amy and the boys, he was able to concentrate on the sermon.

Pastor Nolan was working his way through the book of Matthew and the sermon for that morning was out of chapter 27, where Christ was mocked and crucified. The message was sobering as verses were read describing the way Christ suffered for the sins of man. But as always Pastor Nolan ended his sermon with a word of encouragement. Everyone rose at the end and sang out on the final hymn before being dismissed.

It took Silas a few seconds to see that Carrie had not risen to follow him out of the pew but was in close conversation with Aunt April. He was standing in indecision when April looked up and caught his eye.

"Silas, would it be alright if Carrie comes to lunch today?"

"Sure."

"We'll bring her home later."

"That's fine. Maybe you could stay to supper."

"We'll plan on it unless Amy and the boys are worse."

Silas gave her a wave, smiled at a very sober Carrie, and headed to the wagon.

Later Carrie sat at the small kitchen table in the parsonage suffering from a headache brought on by holding back her tears. She had barely touched her chicken and potato, partly because she'd asked so many questions but also because she was upset over what she'd heard that morning.

"Remember what I said, Carrie, about sin starting in the Garden of Eden? We read about it in the book of Genesis. It was not God's perfect plan for us to sin, but He gave man a choice and since man chose to disobey, man then needed a Savior."

"I understand all of that, Pastor Chad," Carrie spoke and the tears finally spilled out. "But they hit Him and took His clothes off, and I just can't stand it that He had to suffer for my sins."

"Oh, Carrie." April rose from her place and came over to hold the sobbing girl. She let her cry for a time and then since it was obvious she was not going to eat her food, the three of them moved into the parlor where April sat near Carrie holding her hand.

"We feel just like you do, Carrie," April spoke now. "Our sins are the reason our Savior had to die, and we don't deserve His love. But Carrie, His love makes us whole. When we trust in Him, He wipes the slate clean. Every sin and wrong is taken away and hung on the cross. And when we sin after we're saved, the Bible says we are to confess it to know the full measure of forgiveness and fellowship with God."

With wide eyes Carrie looked at Pastor Chad, and he smiled at her in confirmation of his wife's words.

"And it's for anyone, isn't it?"

"Anyone at all," April said with a smile.

"I've counseled many people in my years as a pastor, Carrie, but I've come across few who are as hungry and willing to know Christ as you."

"Does that mean you'll help me—tell me what to do?"

"With pleasure, Carrie."

"Should we get on our knees?" She was very serious now and a little anxious, as if she feared they would change their minds and send her away.

"Of course we can get on our knees," April said, and smiled at her husband who was looking a little doubtful of ever getting off the floor once he knelt down.

When all three were kneeling in front of the sofa, Pastor Chad opened his Bible to Romans 10:9,10. "Read these verses, Carrie."

"'That if thou shalt confess with thy mouth the Lord Jesus, and shalt believe in thine heart that God hath raised him from the dead, thou shalt be saved. For with the heart man believeth unto righteousness; and with the mouth confession is made unto salvation.'"

"Do you understand what you read there, Carrie?"

"I think so. I need to pray and tell God I sin and also tell Him I believe He died for my sins."

"That's right, honey. You pray anytime you want and say what's in your heart."

April was glad that Chad had taken over because she was so choked with emotion that she couldn't have uttered a word. She listened with her heart bursting as Carrie began hesitantly and then with confidence.

"God . . . Jesus . . . I've done sins. And well—I'm sorry You had to die because I've sinned. But even though I sin and I really don't understand it all, I know I need You. I know that You love me and I want You to be with me from now on. I want to confess with my mouth and believe in my heart, and I do, God. Please save me today. And please, God, help Mandy and Clovis and Levi and Becca to believe too, and Pa too, wherever he is. Amen."

There was no sound for a few moments. Finally Pastor Chad looked to find Carrie watching him with her heart in her eyes.

"Did I do it right?" she whispered. He couldn't get any words past the lump in his throat so he just nodded and put his arms gently around her. She hugged him back, and the three of them stayed there and talked for a long time. Carrie's new knowledge of salvation showed on her face as she asked questions with surprising insight.

She couldn't quite stifle a giggle when they finally rose from the floor and Pastor Chad groaned and made faces on the way to his feet.

"Do you suppose, Aunt April, that I could finish my lunch? I'm hungry now."

April was more than happy to see her eat some more. Carrie spent most of the day with them. They played games and not once, Carrie noticed, did they seem tired of her seemingly endless questions about God and the Bible. Both Chad and April were very blessed at how concerned she was over the unsaved state of her family. Before they left for Silas and Amy's they prayed together. All three of them petitioned God on behalf of Carrie's father and siblings.

Silas and Mandy fixed supper that night just to give Amy a break. The boys had not been sick again, but both were very weak. Amy insisted they have broth for supper.

Chad and April did stay for supper, and the meal was relaxed and plentiful. Both Silas and Amy noticed a kind of new rapport between Carrie, Chad, and April. They both assumed it was from spending the afternoon together getting to know each other better.

When Silas had come home without Carrie and described to Amy what had taken place, Amy was concerned. She now wanted very much to ask her if everything was okay, but there was never a private moment and bedtime was upon them before Amy could take a breath. Comforting herself with the fact that Carrie was as cheerful as ever, Amy realized she couldn't have spent time with people more wonderful than Chad and April Nolan.

Amy was falling asleep on this reassuring thought when Carrie knocked on their bedroom door.

"Come in," Silas called.

"Did I wake you?" Carrie's voice sounded excited.

"No. Are you alright?"

"I'm fine. I wanted to tell you that I talked with Pastor Chad and Aunt April today, and I confessed my sins to God and believed on Jesus."

Amy jumped out of bed and threw her arms around Carrie. As soon as she let go, Silas claimed her with a mighty hug that made her squeal and then laugh.

Amy pulled her over to the bed where they all sat and began to talk at once. The words were exuberant, and even though they tumbled out quickly and interrupted each other in excitement, the meaning of the words floated with clarity to Mandy, who stood on the stairway listening.

Mandy was relieved that Carrie wasn't sick, as she had suspected when she heard her leave her room. But neither was she overjoyed at what she was overhearing. It was becoming more and more clear to her every day that Silas and Amy had a very special relationship with God, and now it seemed that Carrie would have it as well.

Mandy made her way silently back to her room. She lay awake for a long time, feeling very lonely and excluded. Somehow she knew that there was something she could do to alleviate the feeling of being left out, but at this moment the answer to the emptiness within eluded her.

25

Preston Culver was the wealthiest man in Baxter. Originally from Reedsburg, Preston, Peter's uncle, had lived in Baxter some 20-odd years. He owned the bank building, the bakery, the largest livery, and three houses. Ross and Peter were moving into the smallest of his houses.

Preston was over 20 years older than his brother Roy, Peter's father. He'd never married and until two years ago, worked for nothing but his bank account, which was plentiful. But a few years ago he developed a severe ulcer, which he didn't recognize as such, and believed himself to be fatally ill. In the weeks of panic before he saw a doctor, he came to grips with the fact that if he died, he was headed to a lost eternity.

Extremely ill and coughing up blood, he made the trip to Reedsburg to his brother's home. Roy, who had prayed for Preston for years, was given the privilege of talking with him and seeing his older brother give his life to God.

There was no anger in Preston when he was told that he was not going to die if he adjusted his eating and work habits. He praised God at having come to Christ and at the chance to live out the rest of his life serving Him.

About a year after Preston's conversion, Peter expressed a desire to move to Baxter. Preston was delighted to take him under his wing. Pete was extremely bright and getting him a job with the bank would have been easy even if Preston hadn't owned the building.

From the day Peter arrived in Baxter, he had lived with Preston in his spacious home on Main Street. But today was moving day for both him and Ross, and Preston was on hand to see the boys off to a good start in their new home.

Ross and Peter had met at church on Ross' first Sunday in town. They had hit it off right away, and when Preston heard their plans to get a place together, he told them he believed he would have a house coming vacant if they would hold off.

Preston, a changed man with the indwelling of Christ, generously gave them a good price on the rent and had the house painted inside and out as well as necessary repairs made before they moved in.

The house was rather compact, with two bedrooms upstairs and a parlor, dining room, and kitchen with a large pantry on the first floor.

Moving began first thing in the morning with two borrowed wagons and many hands to help. Ross had purchased some bedroom furniture from Preston that had to be moved out of the house, along with Pete's belongings and the furniture Preston had given him.

"Uncle Preston, I feel funny about this. You won't have anything left in your parlor."

"No doubt you've noticed how often I entertain," he said sardonically. "You know I'm always in the living room or my study. Now, not another word about it. You boys need this furniture more than I do, and that's the end of it."

Peter and Ross exchanged a shrug over the sofa table they were carrying and continued on to the wagon. It wasn't as if they didn't want the furniture; it just felt a little strange to be clearing out some of the rooms in this man's home.

They worked through the morning until Ross reminded everyone that Grandma Em was expecting them for lunch. No one could argue with that plan. It was a bunch of hungry men who converged upon Grandma Em's.

Sitting around the dining room table they partook of roast beef, potatoes with gravy, peas, hot biscuits, applesauce, and pitchers of ice water and tea. Dessert was strawberries over shortcake, covered with fresh cream.

Ross teased Grandma Em as they rose and said their thanks. "No one will be able to work when we get back to the house, but if I have to finish moving by myself, it was worth it." Kissing her cheek he headed out the door. She turned to find Preston smiling at her.

"Thank you, Emily. Everything was delicious."

"The pleasure was all mine, Preston. And please allow me to thank *you* for what you're doing for the boys. I've begun to think of Ross as my very own, and knowing that he'll be living with Peter and in one of your homes, well, it's a comfort."

"They're good boys and I think they'll be good for each other." Laughing softly before he continued, his dark, expressive eyes sparkled. "Pete has told me that all the girls forget he's there when Ross walks into the room. What I think is so funny is that Ross says the same thing about Pete." They both laughed then and Preston reached out and briefly touched Grandma Em's arm before he joined the men in the wagon.

The work continued a few more hours before Ross and Pete were settled. Excitement radiated from them over this new adventure, and Preston shook his head over their boyish delight.

"Why don't you let me send Cora over here to help you settle? You know she could set things up twice as fast as you boys."

"No, we're fine," they assured him as they headed to their own bedrooms with linens donated by the family.

Again Preston shook his head. These boys had never lived on their own, never cooked or cleaned or taken care of themselves. Although money was no longer a driving force in his life, he said a prayer of thanks that he could afford his housekeeper, Cora, who saw to his comfort.

Ross and Pete couldn't have understood Preston's thoughts until the next morning when Pete could barely swallow the coffee Ross had made. Ross found his eggs raw on one side and nearly burned on the other.

"How did you manage this?" Ross inquired of Pete. But Pete only smiled and said, "Try the coffee." He laughed uproariously at the grimace on Ross' face and the two agreed, in great humor, to walk down to the hotel for breakfast.

26

"Robyn MacDonald, does your mother know where you are?" Mac towered over the small, naked form of his daughter and tried not to laugh. Robyn had meticulously spread her clothing on a nearby rock so as not to get it wet while she played in a round tub that had half filled with rain water during the night.

"I didn't get my dress wet."

"I can see that. But you know better than to take your clothes off when you're outside, Robyn." Trying to sound stern, he knew he was failing. Her little hands fluttered over her tummy, and she kept putting her fingers in her belly button.

"Robyn." Mac heard Julia call just then so he took his daughter's hand to lead her around the corner of the house to her mother. Julia's eyes widened a little at the sight of her unclothed daughter, and she threw her hands out in exasperation.

"She's only been out here a few minutes, Mac. What am I going to do with her?"

Mac didn't answer and Julia saw that he found it all very amusing. His eyes sparkling with mirth nearly started her own laughter, and that would have been a disaster. Calvin and Charles had no such control, and as they came out of the house behind Julia the air was filled with their glee.

"Alright, boys," Mac said when it looked as though they were going to laugh all day. "That's enough. Charlie, will you please go around the house and get Robyn's clothes? And Cal, you go around and get that tub. Don't dump the water, just put it here in front of the house."

The boys did as they were asked, and when Mac had Robyn's clothes in his hands he bent down and put her small cotton underdrawers on her. Charlie went to help with the tub and when he and Cal set it on a level spot of ground, Mac spoke.

"Alright, Robyn. Climb in."

They watched her shiver for an instant as the cool water hit her skin, but the day was a scorcher and she was laughing and splashing within seconds.

Mac had work waiting for him and the boys, but he settled onto the front steps next to his wife and watched his daughter play. Charlie was bent over the tub trying to get Robyn to swim in the shallow water. Cal sat beside his mother.

"I can't get Carrie off of my mind, Mac," Julia said. "April and Pastor Chad must be floating on air."

"I'm sure I would be. You should have seen Si's face when he told me. 'My girl Carrie knows Christ now.' That was just the way he said it."

"I can understand how he feels—all five of them have become a part of us so quickly. It scares me a little because their father isn't back and I just can't think what we'll do if they go away now."

"We'll praise God for the time we've had them and the work He's done in Carrie's life. It's not as if we'll never see them again. We'll have them over, and we'll try to get them to church."

They were quiet for a moment, and then Cal asked, "What time are we supposed to go to the birthday party tonight?"

"Six-thirty."

"Are you all ready, Julia?" The question came from her husband.

"I think so. I wrapped the necklace, and I'll start frying the chicken in a few hours."

"I thought Christine was frying the chicken and you were doing one of the cakes."

"It was that way, but Christine is miserable. The baby has

dropped, and she feels like she can hardly move. I wouldn't be surprised if she had that baby at Carrie's party tonight."

"I thought the birth was a few weeks away."

"It is, but babies have this penchant for making doctors look silly, and they do that by arriving when they want and not when they're supposed to."

They talked a bit more and then the afternoon sped by as they prepared for Carrie Jackson's fifteenth birthday party.

— ✤ —

"Well now, don't you smell nice." Ross ignored him as Pete came into Ross' bedroom. Ross continued to brush his hair into place. Pete reached over and tapped a brightly wrapped package on the dresser. "What did you get her?"

"A brush and comb with a matching mirror."

"That's not very exciting. She's probably been getting hairbrushes on her birthday for years now."

"Not according to Amy. The five of them have one that they all share." The men looked at each other for the space of a few heartbeats. They had both been raised in homes of considerable means, and going without something as mundane as a hairbrush was beyond their realm of comprehension.

"Tell Carrie I said happy birthday." Pete left on those softly spoken words and Ross stared for a few seconds at the empty doorway. It wasn't long before his thoughts turned back to the evening ahead and, as he was coming to expect, Amanda.

It was the strangest sensation, he thought, this odd feeling that God wanted him to befriend Amanda. "Don't You know how vulnerable I am where she is concerned, Lord?" Ross had asked the question out loud one day during his prayer time. But it was still the same—"Get close to Amanda, Ross."

He had no more time to ponder the thought. He knew that if he didn't get to Grandma Em's right now to pick her up they would be late. With a final check in the mirror he picked up the present and descended the stairs.

— ✛ —

"How's this, Mandy?"

"Oh, Carrie, you look so pretty!"

The two girls stood in front of the mirror in Mandy's room and looked at the changes in each other. They were considerably filled out from head to foot. Their faces were fuller and shining with health.

Mandy looked down with satisfaction at the way her small bust finally filled out the front of her dress. With her added weight she and Amy were very near the same size.

Carrie was built much the same as Mandy, petite of height but just a shade slimmer. She looked adorable this evening in her lavender dress with short puffed sleeves and rounded neckline. Amy had helped pull her hair up and the effect was darling with her slim neck and nearly bare arms.

Mandy's dress was light pink and set off the darkness of her hair and eyes. The waistline was nipped in and the bodice fitted. Mandy was thrilled that she no longer looked so straight up-and-down. Her own neckline was modestly rounded with a ruffle around the edge and sleeves longer than Carrie's, but the lightweight cotton fabric made her outfit very cool and comfortable.

"Mandy, I've been wanting to talk with you and I haven't had a chance. Can we talk now?"

"Of course," Mandy answered, even though she knew that Carrie was going to tell her about her new religion. What Mandy didn't know was that the words Carrie had chosen were going to affect her tremendously. They sat on the edge of the bed facing each other.

"We're family, Mandy," Carrie began without warning, speaking quickly lest she lose courage. "And nothing can ever change that. I think we're closer than most sisters, and I wouldn't want it any other way. But I realized after we moved in with Silas and Amy that there was another family I wanted to be part of and that's God's family.

"I don't think there's ever been anything that we haven't shared in, but this—" She stopped for a moment, afraid that Mandy would be angry with her. "This is something we can't share in, Mandy—because you don't think people sin. And I'm telling you, Mandy—you're wrong. I want you to know that I'm praying that you'll understand how wrong you are and come to Jesus."

There were tears in Mandy's eyes, and it was almost too much for Carrie. She knew Mandy was hurt, but her soul was more important than a few earthly tears. "Mandy, I love you," she continued softly. "That won't ever change. Today is my birthday, but I wasn't really born until last Sunday when I told God I needed a Savior."

Mandy was speechless. Carrie's face shone with contentment and peace. This wasn't some religion, some Sunday morning ritual. This was a changed life.

"Will you think about what I've said, Mandy? Think about how much Jesus Christ loves you and what He did on the cross to prove that love."

The older girl nodded almost with relief. They hugged, each with their thoughts in a whirl—Mandy, trying to absorb all that Carrie had said, and Carrie, praying fervently that she'd used the right words, and nearly begging God to save her big sister.

27

"You mean the entire family is coming?" Carrie asked the question in incredulous surprise when she saw the tables Amy had set for supper.

"That's right. You don't turn 15 every day, and that makes it something to celebrate."

"Well now," Silas spoke as he came into the kitchen. "If you aren't a sight for tired eyes." Silas smiled at his adopted family, who sparkled visibly under his words of praise. Rebecca stood quietly in a peach-colored dress and matching pinafore. She didn't notice Silas looking at her because her eyes were fastened on the cake sitting on the sideboard in the kitchen.

The boys were freshly scrubbed, and their plaid shirts and navy blue pants were spotless. Levi already had his shirttail tugged out, but he was still in good shape for the party.

The older girls smiled back at Silas, feeling special under his approving gaze, and then watched as he approached his wife. Amy was in light blue and if the look in Silas' eye was any indication, breathtaking. She stood still under his scrutiny and raised her face for his kiss when he stopped in front of her.

The children were long since used to such displays of affection, and it was obvious to each of them that this couple was in love. Levi and Clovis found the entire episode sickening, whereas Carrie and Mandy thought it was the most wonderful thing on earth. At 15 and 18 they couldn't help but dream of someday having someone like Silas Cameron in love with them. They could even visualize who they wanted that *someone* to be, but there were last minute details to be handled for supper and no more time for daydreams.

— ✤ —

"If everyone has had enough, let's go into the living room for presents. We'll have the cake later. Oh, and leave the dishes."

The family did as Amy bade, and Carrie suddenly found herself the center of attention. Seated in the middle of the sofa with a very pregnant Christine on one side and April on the other, she looked at the low table in front of her, covered with presents. She had never seen so many. And they were all for her!

Biting her lip, Carrie looked up, uncertain of what to do next. The eyes she met were Silas', and he said gently, "Go ahead, honey, start anywhere you want."

She looked at Mandy before reaching for a package and received an encouraging smile.

"Start with this one, Carrie. It's from Pastor Chad and me." Aunt April rescued her by giving her a starting place, and Carrie smiled at her gratefully before tugging the paper from a low, flat package. There was no immediate reaction to the book she unwrapped, until she turned the binding up to see the words—*Holy Bible*.

"Oh, Aunt April!" Carrie cried as she threw her arms around the woman next to her. "Is it really my very own Bible—one I can keep?"

"It's all yours," April spoke through the stranglehold on her neck. Every adult in the room was having trouble swallowing, as they watched Carrie slowly open the Bible. Touching the pages as though they would tear under her lightest touch, Carrie raised her head. Her smile was blinding. She searched out Pastor Chad among the sea of faces.

"Thank you," Carrie said softly, and he nodded from across the room.

The next present was the comb-and-brush set from Ross. Again Carrie beamed at the provider of the gift, touching and looking at it as though there had never been anything more wonderful. She went on to receive a pair of cuticle scissors and two cotton handkerchiefs from

Grandma Em and a small leather coin purse, a box of hair pins, and a string of beads from her sisters and brothers.

Silas and Amy bought her a lovely pair of high-top shoes in jet black leather. They looked like they would be a perfect fit, and again Carrie was thrilled.

The last gift was from the Luke Cameron family, the Mark Cameron family, and the MacDonalds. They had gone in together and bought a tiny gold cross, brightly polished and delicately engraved. It hung on a gold chain.

Amanda, who had been sitting on the floor next to Ross, leaned forward as her sister pulled the chain from the box. Carrie caught her movement, and the girls exchanged astonished looks.

"I can't accept this," Carrie said the words after a moment. "It must have cost a fortune, and I might lose it or something."

"We want you to have it, Carrie. Remember, all three of our families went in together, and none of us think you're likely to lose it." Luke spoke for the group, and Carrie glanced at him before her eyes locked with Mandy's.

There had never been jewelry in the Jackson family. Their mother hadn't even owned a wedding ring. Ross, silent watching the entire exchange, suddenly had the impulse to shower Amanda with jewels. It wasn't financially possible of course, but he desperately wanted to give her something as lovely as the cross—anything to see the look of longing disappear when she received something of her own.

In the silence following Luke's words, Mark moved toward Carrie and gently took the necklace from her hands. Mark worked the clasp, and then Carrie looked down in silent awe as the cherished gift fell to a perfect length for the neckline of her dress.

"Thank you," she said, and met the eyes of each of them. "I'll treasure it always."

Much laughter and talk followed, and Mandy stayed where she was, hoping Carrie would join her. She got her wish and the girls communicated wordlessly as Carrie knelt down in front of her and let Mandy look her fill. Mandy's hand reached out and lifted the tiny cross, her thumb moving carefully over the slight furrows in the gold. She let the cross go and it dropped softly back against Carrie's chest. The girls' eyes met again and they both giggled in delight and threw their arms around each other. The words came then, in a torrent.

"It's so pretty."

"I just love it."

"You mustn't lose it."

"I'll only wear it on Sundays."

"That's a good idea."

"You can wear it, Mandy."

"No, it's yours."

"I know, but you can."

"Oh, Carrie."

They laughed together then because they felt so good and the evening had been so wonderful. Carrie moved off to see someone else, leaving Ross and Amanda alone.

"She got nice things, didn't she?" Mandy said with genuine pleasure.

"Yes, she did. She certainly looked pleased." Ross was once again taken by her selflessness. She didn't seem the least bit jealous of all the gifts and attention her sister was receiving.

"It was thoughtful of you to bring her something, Ross."

"It was my pleasure. Pete said to tell her happy birthday. I forgot to tell her when she was just here."

"Are you two all settled in your house?"

"I think so. We have more furniture than I imagined we would, thanks to Pete's Uncle Preston."

"Preston Culver?"

"Right. Do you know him?"

"I know of him, but then everyone in Baxter can say that. It seems like he owns everything in town."

"I don't think everything, but he's a very successful businessman. He's also a very nice guy. You would probably like him."

"You might be right, but it's doubtful I'll ever meet him."

"He goes to the church, Amanda."

"Oh, I guess I didn't see him."

"Well, I'm sure you'll be at the ceremonies on Wednesday, so I'll have to introduce you."

"I can't believe it's nearly the Fourth of July."

"This will be my first one away from Hayward."

"Do you miss your family?"

"Not as much as I thought I would, but yes, I do miss them."

"And your girlfriend. You must miss her."

Ross looked at her in surprise. Her voice had sounded so resigned, and she was looking at him in a way Ross was not ready to deal with.

"Time to sing and have cake," Silas called from the doorway. Not until Ross had his cake and he and Mandy were separated by many people, did he realize he hadn't told her that he no longer had a girl.

28

"Oh, Luke! That was a bad one," Christine gasped. "You better go for Mark."

"I'm going. I'll run over and ask Amy to sit with you."

"Fine." She gasped again as another contraction seized her. The last had subsided and another had started when Luke's horse raced toward Silas'.

Mandy, having heard the horse approach, was out of her bed and on the stairway when Luke pounded, making her the first to the door.

"I have to go for Mark. Please ask Amy to go over with Christine." He was racing for the horse when Silas' shout stopped him.

"Luke, stay with Christine! I'll go for Mark!" It took a moment for the words to sink in and then Luke was swinging back off the horse and running for his house.

"I'll go over and see if there's anything I can do, Silas. I'll be dressed in a minute."

"Mandy, that's not a good idea. It's not very pleasant for a woman—"

Mandy's laughter stopped him. "Silas, you're forgetting I'm the oldest in my family. I was three years old when I watched Mama have Carrie."

Silas heard her move off in the dark before rushing into Amy to tell her what was going on. Amy was still standing in sleepy surprise at the bottom of the stairs, long after the sound of the horse's hooves had died away.

"Did Silas tell you I was going next door?"

"Oh, Mandy you startled me. Yes, yes he said you were going over. Would you rather I went?"

"No, I'll be fine."

Amy was secretly relieved. She had listened to the

stories her sisters-in-law told, and she wasn't really sure
she wanted to be anywhere near a woman in labor.

— ❖ —

"No one heard me knock, so I came on back."

Both Luke and Christine were vaguely surprised to see
Mandy enter their bedroom, but Christine's labor over-
shadowed everything. At the moment they gave very little
thought to the fact that this young, unmarried woman was
coming to help a woman on the verge of giving birth.

"I told Amy I would come see if I could be of any help.
Luke, we could use a little more light in here." Sounding
distracted, she moved toward the bed, all her concentration on Christine. She bent over the bed and put her hand
beneath Christine's back. The contraction subsided and
Mandy smiled at the older woman.

"They're coming hard, aren't they?"

"I want to push."

"No, Christine! Don't push, do you hear me?" It was a
command. "Now, you're nearly suffocating in these covers." She turned to Luke who was coming in with another
lamp. "We need some sheeting and a light blanket."

Luke moved to obey and then sat on the bed by Christine
and watched in fascination as Mandy readied the room.
Mark's nurse, Maggie, always took care of this, and Luke
realized that he would not have known what to do.

"Have the wash basin ready. I washed up in the kitchen
but Mark will want to wash up in here." Luke only sat
staring. "Please, Luke, take care of it."

After that Mandy forgot he was in the room. She sat with
Christine and talked with her, bathed her face, and sup-
ported her when contractions came.

"Mandy, I have to push."

"No!" The word was shouted and Mandy whipped back
the sheet to check on her patient. "Christine," she said in a
voice almost angry with concern. "Don't push! You want

Mark here to bring this baby into the world. Now just hold on a little bit longer."

But there was no answer from the woman on the bed whose eyes were dilated with pain, a woman who was losing the battle with her body and had to push this baby out or die, she was sure.

"I can see the head!" Mandy wailed. "Try to hold on Christine, please!" Mandy, intent on Christine and the baby, didn't hear Mark enter the room and quickly scrub his hands. Quickly deciding not to move Mandy, he merely bent over beside her and gave Christine a few instructions. When the next contraction hit, a tiny baby girl slid into his waiting arms.

"It's a girl, Christie," Luke said from his place beside her as he tried to see more of the new little miracle God had given them.

Mark and Mandy's hands worked in easy rhythm and in moments the smallest Cameron was dried and wrapped in a clean, warm sheet. A few moments later Maggie Pearson, Mark's full-time nurse, was ushered to the door by Silas. Mandy, seeing she was no longer needed, slipped quietly from the room. Silas had gone to the kitchen, but Mandy walked past him without a word.

"Mandy?"

"I'm going back to the house."

Silas walked behind her out the door and watched her stop in the yard. He followed her off the porch and down the steps and came up beside her. The moon, just a sliver in the sky, kept him from seeing her face, and he wondered what she was thinking.

"What kind of God can make a perfect little baby like that and then take the mama of five children when they need her so badly? What kind of God can keep their pa away, so that they wait and wonder all the time and can't be sure about tomorrow?

"Amy's uncle talks about God's love, but He doesn't love everyone the same. He's given something to Carrie that I can't have. He's hiding something special from me and I can't find it. He doesn't want me to find it."

"That's not true, Mandy," Silas said quietly and then was afraid to go on. She was exhausted, the note of hysteria in her voice told him that. He believed they should discuss this after she'd had a full night's sleep.

"I'm tired," she said suddenly. "I have so many questions, but I just can't think straight."

"Let's go home." Taking her arm, he felt as well as heard her first sob. She was crying in earnest by the time they reached the house.

Carrie and Amy met them at the back door. Amy looked to Silas in near panic, thinking something had happened to Christine. Silas told her quickly that they had a niece but that Mandy needed to be put to bed.

Carrie helped Mandy undress and in no time at all she was cleaned up and in her own bed. Carrie, worried about her sister, climbed in beside her. They were both asleep very quickly.

Silas, downstairs in bed with his wife, spoke just as they went off to sleep. "Tomorrow is the Fourth, so Luke and I will do no more than feed. Then Mandy and I are going to take a drive. She has questions and I hope I have answers. Either way I've got to talk to that girl about things that just won't wait."

29

"It won't work, Silas. We have a million things to do to get ready for this afternoon. Plus Josh and Kate are here as well, and I can't abandon Amy."

Mandy sailed off in the direction of the kitchen, leaving Silas in frustration. She had been so receptive to the idea of a drive. When he had mentioned talking over her questions about God she was thrilled, almost astounded that he really cared that much. But when he suggested they leave right then, Mandy had not even hesitated in her reply.

"There is so much to do. But thank you for thinking of me."

"We're not going to be gone all day. In fact, we could just take a walk."

"It won't work, Silas," she had begun, and Silas had not known what to do. *Maybe it's my will,* Silas thought, *and not God's will that we talk. I'll have to leave it for now.*

Everyone was going to Grandma Em's for a Fourth of July supper and then to the edge of town for the fireworks display. Josh and Kate were at Silas and Amy's to give Christine and the baby some quiet, and Mandy was right, there were many things to do.

There was a lull in the activity just after lunch when Luke came to get Kate to put her down for a nap.

"Mandy, would you mind coming over with me? Christine wants to talk with you."

"Sure, I can come." Mandy was pleased, not because she felt she deserved any thanks but because she wanted to see the baby.

Luke led the way into the bedroom and then left the women alone.

"Come on over," Christine called from the bed. Mother and baby were snuggled together since Christine had just fed her. "Sit here on the bed so you can get a closer look."

"Oh, she's lovely."

"We think so." Christine looked tired but very content. "Would you like to hold her?"

"Please," Mandy said with a delighted smile.

Christine noticed she handled her like a mother of ten, supporting her back and head and keeping her well covered. She crooned softly into the tiny face, and Christine thought how sweet and giving she was. Luke rejoined Christine on the bed and spoke.

"We want to thank you for coming over last night; you were wonderful and I really needed you."

"You're welcome. I was glad to help. What did you name her?"

"Rachael, after Christine's mother."

"Rebecca was almost a Rachael. It's such a pretty name."

"Her full name is Rachael *Amanda* Cameron."

Mandy's head came up slowly on the emphasis of her name. She looked at Luke to see if he was serious, then to Christine whose smile was very watery.

"Am I the Amanda?" She whispered the words.

"We know no other."

"Oh my," she breathed the words and cuddled the sleeping infant even nearer. With almost a reverence she kissed the miniature forehead below the wisps of dark hair. Closing her eyes, she laid her cheek against the downy little head.

"It's such an honor, I mean I didn't do that much, that is, nothing that anyone wouldn't have done in my—" She stopped when they laughed.

"Mandy obviously didn't see you standing there like a man lost, Luke, or she wouldn't say that."

"I *was* a man lost. We had more time with Josh and Kate, and Maggie was there to get everything ready."

As if the mention of Josh's name could conjure him up, he appeared at the door, tears in his eyes.

"Can I come home now?"

"What's happened, honey?" his mother asked. Josh glanced at Mandy and didn't say anything.

"Was it Levi or Clovis?" Mandy asked with resignation.

"Levi," the boy admitted.

"What did he do?"

"I don't know. It's like he's mad at me and I don't know what I did."

"Lee is not very patient, not that that excuses him. You probably didn't do anything. Think of poor Clovis, he gets it all the time."

"Does your aunt or uncle know you left?" Luke asked.

"No."

"Well, head back over and tell them I said you can come home. And if there is something you need to clear up with Levi, you'd best do it."

"I have to go," Mandy said. "I'll make sure everything is okay." She handed the baby to Luke's outstretched hands and marveled at how small he made her seem. Their father had never been around when any of them were born. It was a new thing to see a man holding an infant with such tenderness.

"Thank you again. I'm more honored than I can say."

"Thank *you*, Mandy. God knew you were just what we needed."

— ❖ —

God knew you were just what we needed. The words kept swarming around in Mandy's head. She almost wished she and Silas had gone for that ride. Luke and Christine made it sound like God had sent her there. Well maybe He had. After all, He was the reason she couldn't get to sleep. Questions repeatedly echoed in her mind over what Carrie had said before the party.

And then after the baby was born she felt such an awful ache inside of her. Having something happen to little Rachael would not have brought her mother back, nor would Mandy have chosen that, even if it would have. But it all seemed so unfair. Her mother was gone, never to return, leaving a terrible void in her world. And Luke and Christine—their life seemed so complete, as if God thought they were extra special and He couldn't think of enough gifts to shower them with.

"Mandy, are you okay?"

"What did you say, Carrie?"

"I said are you okay? You've been real quiet since you came back from seeing the baby. You're happy that she's named after you, aren't you?"

"Oh, I think it's wonderful. I guess I'm a little tired."

Leaving her to her thoughts, Carrie didn't question her sister anymore. They continued to load the wagon for Grandma Em's without further conversation.

30

"I would say we worked very hard. In fact I'm not sure I'll have any energy left for tonight."

"In that case we'll get the lemonade." Ross and Pete disappeared into the kitchen as Grandma Em sank down into one of the chairs in the backyard. It took her a moment to realize that Preston was staring at her from his place in another yard chair. She immediately interpreted the look.

"I was only kidding, Preston. I'm fine."

"Are you?" He didn't sound convinced.

"I'm tired, but I'm not going to collapse or anything quite so dramatic."

"I want to see you taking it easy tonight."

"Oh, you do, do you?" She was clearly amused but tried not to smile when she saw how serious he was.

"Yes, I do. And if you don't, I just might have to have a talk with Luke or Mark about the way their grandmother over-does when they're not looking."

"You wouldn't dare!"

"Just try me, Emily." He smiled then, tempted to tell her he liked the way she looked when she was a bit outraged. But even with as little as he knew about women, he was certain that would get him into all kinds of trouble.

She eyed him then to gauge just how serious he had been, and he returned her gaze, telling her with his smiling eyes that he would do just as he said. She couldn't help but smile back at him, so charming was his grin.

The boys came back carrying the pitcher of lemonade and four glasses. With great ceremony they served their elders, and when everyone had quenched their thirst the boys began to bring some of the food from the kitchen to the tables they had set up earlier.

As the families began to arrive and saw the tables set up outside, everyone's spirits soared. Silas and Amy's wagon, filled with their own five plus Josh and Kate, looked as though it had enough children to fill the schoolhouse.

Mandy helped fill little hands with baskets full of food, making her one of the last to come away from the wagon. She had just begun to lift a basket full of pies when she heard Carrie say, "Hi Ross. Hi Pete." At that same instant she realized the basket was too heavy for her. The last thing she wanted to do was behave like a helpless woman in front of Ross. She just hated it when girls acted like that; it was deceitful. So against her better judgment she lifted the basket.

The weight nearly staggered her, and she had just steadied herself when Ross stepped forward and took the basket from her.

"Whatever you do Amanda, don't ask for help." His voice was laced with annoyed sarcasm. Mandy felt rebuked and foolish. Ross walked away and Mandy felt her face flush with heat. She was sure Pete and Carrie had heard him. Pete relieved Carrie of her jug of cider, and they moved toward the house.

Mandy stood staring into the empty wagon bed without really seeing it. A shadow passed over her, drawing her attention up to an older, distinguished-looking man beside her.

"Is everything unloaded?" His voice was deep and pleasant and Mandy nodded yes.

"Well then, I'll escort you to supper." He held his arm out, but Mandy only stared at it. "How presumptuous of me; we haven't been introduced. I'm Preston Culver and you are . . . ?" He left the question hanging, knowing exactly what the response would be.

"Mandy Jackson."

"May I please escort you to supper, Mandy?"

"Thank you," she said with a grateful smile as she placed her hand in the crook of his arm. She did not see Ross or Pete watching them, but Preston gave them both a very pointed look as they passed, clearly communicating that one of *them* should have escorted her.

Not needing to be told twice, Ross maneuvered himself carefully, and to Mandy's chagrin, sat across from her at the table. The meal was half over before she even looked at him and then immediately away. Ross felt panicked. For the first time she was uncomfortable with him. He hadn't meant to be so abrupt with her, and he was going to apologize—but something was different this time. He had hurt her. Something he hadn't believed to be possible with the way she seemed to accept every harsh word or act that came into her world.

He determined to corner her after supper and even ask her to sit with him at the fireworks display. But she busied herself in the kitchen right after the meal, and Ross paced around outside in an effort to get near her.

"Ross, can you get the door for me?" It was Susanne holding a meat platter in each hand. Ross jumped at the chance.

Once inside, he saw that Mandy's hands were not in the dish water or even drying the dishes. She was making trips to the dish cabinet in the dining room and putting dishes and hollowware away.

"I seem to keep repeating myself and at some point you're not going to believe me, but I *am* sorry about the way I spoke to you, Amanda."

Placing the dish on the shelf, Mandy looked up into Ross' eyes as he stood next to the tall cabinet where he'd followed her. Mandy, as usual, truthfully revealed to Ross what she was thinking.

"I just hate it when women play games in order to get attention. I knew the basket was too heavy for me, but I figured you would think asking for help was an act. So I lifted it, even though I knew better."

"I don't know you very well, Amanda," *not as well as I'd like to*, he thought, "but if there's one thing I have learned since meeting you, it's that there's no pretense in you. If you had asked for help with the basket, I'd have known instantly that it was genuine desire for help and not a female ploy."

"I'm glad you know that I'm honest. It's important to me."

"I wondered if you would sit with me tonight during the fireworks?"

"I'd like that, Ross, but the truth is I feel a little funny about your girlfriend. I mean, I didn't think you meant anything permanent or anything," she rushed to assure him. "But I just don't think it's fair to her."

"Sarah and I have no plans for the future. She's free to see whomever she wants and the same goes for me."

"Oh."

Again Ross was not ready to handle what he saw in her eyes. There was no way he was going to love this woman. She was not a Christian and no matter how sweet she was, or how much she needed protection, until she made a decision for Christ, and only God knew when that would be, Ross *had* to keep his distance.

"Excuse me, Amanda, I might be needed outside. I'll let you get back to work." Ross left, thinking that he'd made a mistake. He knew he was supposed to keep his distance, and yet he'd asked her to be with him for the rest of the evening. He honestly couldn't figure out why God would ask him to get close to Amanda unless he was supposed to talk to her about the Lord. For some reason the thought had never occurred to him before. He decided then and there that he would do exactly that.

31

"Couldn't this have waited?"

"What for?"

The wizened man shrugged. "I didn't really care to come all the way from Reedsburg in the heat. And some of us take holidays off."

"I never take days off. It's not good for business. Besides, with everyone tied up with the celebrations, no one will notice you coming and going. Have you got what you need?"

"Of course. What's the name?"

Aaron Marks held out an official document to display the name at the bottom.

"If you've got his name on a contract, what do you need me for?"

"Only a fool would sign the one you're going to forge and Jackson is no fool. This old contract is for the job he's on now. But this new one will be binding nonetheless and I'll have what I want."

"I don't care to hear about the details. Have you got the money?"

A bag of coins hit the desk. The little man looked them over, put the bag in his pocket, and went to work.

— ⁂ —

The town had a great time at the fireworks display. The evening began with several children reciting poems or stories about the freedoms their nation enjoyed. After dark, the fireworks commenced. Some were shot into the air and others, attached to poles, lit up the ground in all their patriotic glory.

Ross and Mandy saw very little of it. Ross had wasted no time after the speeches to ask Mandy a little bit about herself. He quickly led the conversation around to eternity and was surprised to find out how knowledgeable she was.

"I know that Carrie has made a decision for Christ and I'm happy for her, but it's as if God is hiding from me."

"You mean, you feel like you're searching and He won't let you see Him?"

"Yes, that's the way it feels. I'm learning a lot from Carrie and at church though, and there are things in the Bible that I didn't know were there, but I almost feel as though the time isn't right. I wonder if it will ever be."

"Have you ever thought of asking God to help you believe, to help you know?"

"No, I'm not used to having anyone help me and it feels foreign. Maybe it's pride but I've always figured I should do things myself—I have up till now."

"And how about after this life? How will you help yourself in eternity?"

"I think I've been a good person, Ross, and that's got to count for *something*." She said the word almost desperately.

"Amanda, I can understand what a blow it is to find out that all the things you've done so far don't count for eternity. The Bible says all our good works are like filthy rags. But look at it this way, if you can't *do* anything to gain salvation, then you can't *do* anything to lose it. I don't know about you, but that's a real comfort to me.

"If all that counted for eternity was the good I've done on this earth then I'd be terrified to die, wondering all the time if I had been good enough to get into heaven. I'll take a sure thing anytime, and believe me, Amanda, salvation through Jesus Christ is a sure thing."

Mandy was soaking in his every word. Ross answered her questions as best he could and quoted many verses to her. But when he asked her if she wanted to pray, she said she wasn't ready.

"I won't push you, Amanda, but the Bible also says that now is the day of salvation. Please know that I'll be praying for you every day. If there's anything I can do to help, just ask."

When things broke up, Mandy thanked Ross for all the time he'd taken with her, and then went to check on her family. Silas, who had seen them talking, was given a brief chance to ask Ross how she was doing.

"She said she needs more time. I have to lean on the verse that says if we seek Him He will be found, because she is seeking and I'm praying she will find Him soon."

"Thanks, Ross. Amy and I are praying, too, and I believe as you do that it's only a matter of time before she comes to Christ."

— ✛ —

"Is it your woman's time, Mandy?" Carrie asked her sister in exasperation. "You're a grouch this morning."

"I am not." The words were empty and without conviction because Mandy knew Carrie was right. She'd had a terrible night and now this morning she was nearly impossible to live with.

"I think I'll go for a walk."

There was plenty of work to do—wet laundry waiting to be hung, pans of bread dough waiting their turn in the oven, and bedding to be aired and changed—but Amy said nothing. This was a girl fighting God. Amy knew from experience that fighting God was miserable and a losing battle. Maybe some time alone was exactly what Mandy needed.

— ✛ —

"I would be terrified to die, wondering all the time if I'd been good enough to get into heaven." Ross had said something like that to Mandy, and she couldn't get the words out of her head.

She had walked a ways from the house and barn and now lay on a grassy knoll with the sun in her face. She touched her warm cheeks and knew she should have grabbed her bonnet. Rolling over onto her stomach, Mandy watched her fingers as they played with the grass and weeds. All that Ross, Carrie, Amy, and Silas had said was running through her mind, and Mandy felt like she was choking with the need to understand and share what they had.

Ross had said to ask God for the understanding. Somehow she felt she had to come to that place *before* God would accept her. But maybe she was wrong. It would seem she was because so far it wasn't working. She wasn't understanding anything.

"Please help me to know You. The Bible says we all sin and I can see now that it's true. I do sin." The words were whispered on the wind and for the first time Mandy felt like God was listening."

"Did you really die for everyone, God—for me too?" These words came on a sob and Mandy's tears fell on the grass beneath her. She told God everything through those tears, her doubts and fears, her pride and stubbornness, but mostly how much she wanted to know Him and how afraid she was that He would turn her away.

She sat up when she had finished praying and stared up at the sky. She wasn't sure why but she suddenly knew that God would never reject her.

No words would come then, but she realized she had crossed over the barrier in her mind. Verses Ross had quoted came to her, and every time one did she said *yes* to God. Yes to believing on His Son. Yes to eternal life. Yes to confessing her sin. And yes to being His child for evermore.

Her tears were spent as a deep peace settled within her. She looked up at the clouds and thought how God Himself had made them. She was on her feet in the next instant and running for the house.

"Carrie!" she shouted as she hit the back door. "Carrie! Amy! Where are you?"

"Mandy what is it? What's happened?" Carrie and Amy bolted into the kitchen at the same time, wide-eyed with fear. They had been in the living room praying for Mandy and hearing her shout their names scared them half to death.

What they saw, as they stared at Mandy's flushed face, made their hearts overflow. Gone was the look of despair and unsureness on her face. In its place was peace and the knowing look of a person who need not fear for tomorrow.

Amy spoke past the lump in her throat as her eyes filled with tears. "Welcome home, Mandy."

"Thanks, Amy," she said as her own tears began. "It's so good to finally be here."

32

The month of July sped by with alarming speed, and before anyone could take a breath it was the middle of August. In that time Mandy and Carrie developed a special routine with Silas and Amy. Each evening after the younger children were asleep, the four of them would sit down at the kitchen table to study the Bible. Silas led the study as they worked their way through the book of Galatians.

First reading a few verses, sometimes only one, Silas, and often Amy, would explain to the girls what God was saying to Christians and how they could apply it to their lives.

One night when they were just finishing and it was time for prayer, Silas told the girls something that had been on his heart for a few weeks.

"It's been wonderful praying with you girls, and I'm blessed each time you remember to pray for your family's salvation. But I've noticed you don't often pray for yourselves. Amy and I pray for you, but I don't want you to be afraid to ask God for things.

"So, beginning tonight I'm going to ask God to show you, in His time, who He has for life mates for you girls." It took a few seconds for that to sink in.

"You mean husbands?"

Carrie's voice was so astounded that Amy laughed. "Silas doesn't mean right now, Carrie."

"Definitely not right now—maybe never. But if and when the time comes—and Mandy, with your being 18, it might be sooner than you think—you'll want God's leading because it's a most important decision; certainly not one to be taken lightly."

The girls looked at one another, and Carrie could see that Silas' words were not that great of a surprise to Mandy.

She would have been amazed if she'd known all of her older sister's thoughts. Mandy never once let on that she was in love with Ross Beckett. Yet privately, any talk of marriage immediately conjured up his face in her mind.

She hadn't seen too much of him lately and had an uncomfortable feeling as to why. It was obvious Ross had been concerned about her soul, and for that Mandy was grateful, but anything beyond, such as a romantic attachment, was plainly out of the question.

Mandy clearly remembered the Sunday she had told him she'd understood and believed in Christ. He'd impulsively hugged her, and Mandy thought her heart would burst. But he hadn't been around much after that. She'd see him at church but not usually close enough to talk with him, and only one Sunday did he come to Grandma Em's for dinner.

Mandy would have held out hope, even through all of those signs, but the day she'd driven into town with Amy and saw Ross walking down the street with Candy Hunter was the day she decided to stop loving Ross Beckett. How naive she had been. If only it was as easy to do as it was to say.

"Now I don't want you to take what I've said as a subtle way of telling you I want you married and out of the house," Silas cut into Mandy's painful thoughts.

"We didn't think that," Mandy told him with a smile.

"Good. Now I think we best get to prayer because my wife is falling asleep." Amy was drooping and didn't argue with his statement.

— ✣ —

"It's a good thing I wasn't in bed. You're making enough noise to wake the dead."

"I tripped on something inside the door. I think the rug is turned up."

"How's Candy?"

Ross didn't answer.

"Ross, how many times do I have to tell you I don't care for her that way? She asked you to supper. I don't think you're moving in on my gal because Candy isn't my gal. What I do think is that you're seeing her to keep your mind off another young lady in town, and that's not fair to you, Candy, or anyone else."

"What's that supposed to mean?" Ross called up to his housemate, who had turned from his place on the stairs and gone up to his room. Ross checked the front door and ran up the stairs behind Pete. He didn't bother knocking but just opened the door and leaned on the jamb.

"What did that cryptic little remark mean?"

"Let me see now," Pete looked up at the ceiling as though picturing the events in his mind. "First you're praying for Mandy because you know she's not saved. Then you spend the Fourth with her and talk to her about Christ. The next day she makes a decision and tells you on the following Sunday that a lot of what you said helped her to that point. You go to Grandma Em's one Sunday after that, and now you're having Sunday dinner with Uncle Preston and myself. When you're at church you're careful to keep as many people as possible between you and Miss Jackson.

"Ross, old buddy, you're avoiding Mandy Jackson like the plague, and I wish I knew why."

"I wish I did, too."

"Now it's your turn to explain your cryptic remark."

"Pete do you have any idea of what it's like to have a girl look at you the way Mandy looks at me?"

"It's probably the same way Carrie looks at me when she thinks I don't notice."

"Carrie? She's 15!"

"Tell me about it."

They were both silent then; there didn't seem to be anything else to say. Both young men sought their rest with hearts full of questions about the future.

33

"I feel like I haven't seen you for days."

"That's why I came in a little early from the barn. We have two more buyers coming in this afternoon, so I'll be tied up again."

"I hate to ask you this, Si," Amy said with her arms around her husband, "but the boys want to be with you so badly, and I can't get them to stand still and try on some pants. School starts in two weeks."

"We'll take care of it right after lunch."

They were just finishing with their food when Silas announced that the boys would try on some clothes immediately following the meal.

"But we want to go with you to the barn," Clovis' eyes pleaded with Silas to say yes.

"You can go to the barn with me, just as soon as you stand still for Amy *and* with a good attitude."

The boys were careful not to reveal their boredom and were in new pants in the living room when Mandy answered a knock on the front door.

"Pa!"

Amy's eyes met those of Silas' where he sat in a chair with Becca. A look of resignation passed between them.

"I found your note, Mandy. Where's your ma?"

"Please, Mr. Jackson, come in." Silas arrived at the door on those words and Mandy was spared, for a few moments, the agony of telling her father that her mother was dead.

"I'm Silas Cameron and this is my wife, Amy. Would you like to sit down?"

The hard-looking man glanced down at his dusty clothing and declined. "I'll stand."

It was a pitiful scene. The children standing silent and unsure of themselves, and Silas and Amy desperately wanting to convey friendship to this man without forcing him to conclude that they were stealing his children. Mr. Jackson was clearly uncomfortable in this house and room. His eyes darted warily between Silas and his oldest daughter.

"Where's your ma, Mandy? Why're you here?"

"She's dead, Pa." The words were whispered. "Silas and Amy were worried about us staying alone and asked us if we wanted to stay here. I didn't know what else to do, so I said yes."

When Ward Jackson did nothing more than stare at Mandy, as if her words were incomprehensible, Mandy went to him and placed her hand on his coat sleeve.

"Pa?"

"When—how did she die?" Her touch seemed to jolt him.

"It was in June. She just got real sick and couldn't get out of bed. It was over fast. The sheriff couldn't find you."

"I've been out West."

"We'll get our things, Pa, and come home with you. Just give us a few minutes."

But the hard-bitten man did not acknowledge her statement. He moved and sat down in the nearest chair. "It was all going to be so different this time. I had plans, and things were going to be different for your ma and me."

The words were spoken to no one in particular, and Silas stepped forward and put his hand on Ward's shoulder.

"We're very sorry about your wife, and we wanted to do what we could. But your family can have their things gathered very quickly and go with you."

The words removed some of the cloud that seemed to have settled over the grieving man, and he looked to each of his children. Rebecca stood uncertain by the chair she'd shared with Silas and gave her pa a small smile when his eyes met hers.

"Hi, Pa." Clovis spoke the words softly when his father looked to him, but Levi, his hands at his sides, did nothing more than return his pa's stare. Carrie moved her hands self-consciously when her father's eyes swung to her and said hello in a voice that sounded strained, especially to her own ears.

Mandy was the last to come under his scrutiny. She saw how tired and how much older he appeared. She also understood for the first time how little they knew this man; it was like meeting a stranger.

"You look like your ma when she was young. The way she looked when I first met her." His head moved to take them all in once again and then rested briefly on Amy.

"They all look good, real good. I thank you for seeing after my younguns."

"It was our pleasure."

"Well, the truth is I hadn't planned to be in town very long." It was obvious to everyone this was a spur-of-the-moment decision.

"They're welcome to stay with us for as long as they need," Silas broke in quickly, wanting this man to know exactly where they stood.

"It might be for the best if they stayed then, I mean with me moving on and all. There's no problem with that is there?"

"No, Pa," Mandy answered when he addressed the question to her. "Only—if you want us to come, we will." Her eyes swept over her siblings and they all nodded. This had been discussed before and each child knew their place was with their pa.

"No, this is best. You look good. I'll probably stop and see you before I go. Was she buried proper?"

"Yes, Pa. At the cemetery. Pastor Nolan said the words. Lots of people came, and it was real nice." Mandy couldn't go on. Her heart ached for this man, and she knew if she had to stand there much longer and watch his broad shoulders droop much lower she was going to start to cry.

Two months ago she'd have screamed at him for not being there when they needed him. Her heart was changed now, and all she felt was deep compassion for this man who seemed not to have the slightest idea how to be a husband and father.

"I'll go now. You all behave."

Mandy and Carrie walked him to the door and the look of surprise on his face when they both went up on tiptoe to kiss his cheek was enough to start their tears. Tears he misinterpreted.

"Don't cry now. It's better this way. Your ma would be glad to know you're doing fine. I'll be in touch."

They stood and watched as he mounted an ill-used nag and rode away without a backward glance.

34

The sun was sinking low in the sky by the time Ward Jackson finished the letter to his daughter. He banged on the doorjamb of the general store for a few minutes before a woman let him in.

"Can't you see the sign? We're closed!" The words, said in exasperation, were ignored.

"I need to post a letter."

"Come back tomorrow."

"I'm leaving town tonight."

"Oh, alright," the woman said with ill-disguised irritation.

A few minutes later, Ward was back astride his nag and headed for home. He had a few things to do, and then he'd put Baxter behind him. Everywhere he looked he saw his wife's face. He *had* to get out of town, fast.

The house had a cold feeling about it, and Ward felt no comfort in the familiar surroundings. He wasted no time in being about his business. Within seconds he had the tools he needed, and was headed off to a rocky place among the bluffs to the west of his few acres.

"When did he get into town?"

"Just this afternoon."

"Where is he now?"

"He headed toward his house."

Aaron Marks said nothing and gave no indication that he was even aware of the other man leaning against the bar.

"Are you going to follow him?"

"I don't know if there's any point in that."

"I wouldn't be so sure about that, Mr. Marks. He just

mailed a letter to someone and said he was headed out of town."

Aaron Marks looked at his informant with new respect. He put his hand out then and shook the other man's hand. No one saw the bills that passed during that casual shake. Just as casually, Aaron Marks made his way to the door and out onto the dark streets of town.

Ward Jackson walked back to his house. He was sweating and his hand was cut from the splintered handle of the shovel, but he was satisfied. His wife would have been proud. He felt a deep pang within him as he pictured his children in the fancy room of the Cameron home, but instantly told himself it was the best thing for them. His wife would have wanted the best for them. He was rounding the corner of the building with the pick and shovel still over his shoulder when a shadow moved in the yard.

"I'm disappointed, Ward. I somehow thought you'd come to see me the moment you were in town."

"There wasn't much point. Your claim was worthless. I didn't find a thing."

"Is that a fact? And I suppose you've been out working in your garden with that shovel."

"Are you calling me a liar?" The voice was deadly. For a moment Marks knew real fear and questioned his own action of coming out here alone.

"The truth is, Marks, I did strike it rich," Jackson went on casually. "But I meant it when I said it wasn't on your claim. I won what was believed to be a worthless stake in a poker game, and it was on that stretch of creek that I struck it rich."

"You're lying." The words were spat out through clenched teeth.

To Marks' surprise, Ward laughed. "You don't like to be wrong, do you Marks? Well, you are. Just think of all the people you must have cheated over the years and call yourself even." As if he hadn't a care in the world, Ward swung the tools down and leaned them against the house.

He heard Marks move, but never suspecting violence from this man, was unprepared for the blow of the shovel on the side of his head. The weight of his body pushed the partially opened door wide and Ward Jackson died on the threshold of his run-down shack.

— ✛ —

"Aaron, we were just looking for you. We need your money in this poker game." The men around the table laughed, and Aaron Marks pulled out a chair and joined them.

"Where'd you go? We had to wait the game for ya."

"A man's got to answer the call of nature sometimes." The words were said with good humor and again the laughter around the table was too loud, the result of "a few too many." Had the vision of the men been a little less blurred, they might have noticed the ashen complexion of Marks' face, and how his hand shook as he lifted his glass to drink and then picked up his cards.

35

Mid-morning of the next day, Luke and Silas were working with a buyer from Delton. A bit of light dickering over the price of a mare was taking place when Silas looked up to see Rufus Collins entering the barn. Silas met him near the door, and the men spoke in quiet tones.

"What's happened, Rufus?" With his heart pounding, Silas asked the question directly. The look on the face of Baxter's sheriff was foreboding.

"Ward Jackson was murdered sometime last night—hit over the head with a shovel. Sorry to tell you like this, Silas, but I knew you'd want to be the one to tell those kids."

"Who would do such a thing?" Silas was stunned.

"We don't have any suspects at this point. Jackson had just arrived back in town."

"We knew he was here because he came by yesterday looking for his wife and kids."

"I never did locate him. How'd he know to come here?"

"Mandy left a note for him at their house."

"So he knew about his wife?"

"No, Mandy told him after he got here. He decided to leave the kids with us. He told us he was headed back out of town and that he'd be in touch."

"When was this?"

"Just after lunch. When do you think he died?"

"I can only assume but I'd say not too long after sundown. The palm of one hand was cut and the shovel laying next to him had a splintered handle."

"What would he have been digging?"

"Your guess is as good as mine."

"Who found him?"

"Aaron Marks."

"Aaron Marks?"

"Yeah. Said he had business with Jackson and heard he was back in town. Said when he went out there this morning to see him, there he was—dead on the doorstep." They talked for a few minutes more, and then Rufus headed back into town.

Silas was caught off guard when Mandy came out to the barn only a few minutes after he'd left.

"Why was the sheriff here, Silas? Has something happened to my pa?" Her face told him she suspected the worst.

"He's dead, Mandy." Silas said the words gently, wishing he'd had more time.

"Oh, Silas, no! He just got back. We didn't get to see him at all!" Silas reached forward and drew her into his arms. He saw that Luke had discreetly taken their customer to the far side of the barn. Silas led a crying Mandy over to a nearby bench.

"How? What happened?" she spoke through her tears.

"It was at your house. He was hit with a shovel."

She was again overcome. Silas would have given anything to spare her the gruesome details, but they were going to come out sooner or later and it was best she hear it from him.

"I was hanging up some laundry when I saw the sheriff ride away. I knew, I just knew, something awful had happened." She worked at composing herself. "What am I going to tell Becca and the boys? Carrie will be okay, but how will I ever explain it to them?"

Silas had no answers for her at the moment. He was sitting beside her, holding her hand, when Luke approached. Silas explained in as few words as possible. Luke suggested, with his eyes on Mandy's white face, that he go for Mark.

"No, I'll be okay. I just need a few minutes before I go in to see Carrie and the kids," she answered for Silas.

"Why don't you let me tell them?"

"Thank you, Silas, but I think I should be the one."

"Why is Mandy crying?" The question came from Clovis, who with Levi suddenly darted into the barn. Mandy was given as little time to adjust as Silas had been given.

"We know you said you had to see a buyer, Silas, but we saw him leave and thought it was okay to come in." Levi said these words, a little intimidated by the serious look on the big man's face.

"Come here, boys." Levi and Clovis unquestioningly obeyed their sister. There were still some tears on her face but Mandy's voice was clear as she reached out and touched them, explaining what had transpired.

Silas thought if he lived to be a hundred, he would never forget the look on Levi's face when he found out that his father was dead. Neither boy cried, but while Clovis was understandably upset and even a little confused, Levi, after a momentary look of pain, visibly built a wall around himself. His expression became very guarded.

"I suppose you're going to tell me *this* was God's will."

"Levi," his sister said almost sternly, upon hearing the cynicism in his young voice. "There were years of hurting before I understood how much God cares for me, and I'm hurting right now, but Levi, I have hope, something I never had before I trusted in God. Pa is dead and I can't change that, but I do know that God still loves us and always will."

For an instant her eyes dared him to refute her, then she grabbed him and hugged him to her fiercely. His sturdy brown arms went around her neck and he held on as though for his life.

After a moment Mandy's arms opened and Clovis was pulled into their circle. There were more tears, many of them, but Mandy spoke to them tenderly and held them close. Luke and Silas, looking on, could only marvel at the special way she had with them and the tremendous love that obviously filled her heart for her young brothers.

36

Everything was strangely familiar and Mandy felt like her heart would burst as she looked at yet another pine box, this one holding her father.

It was the morning of the next day and she'd had to remind the children that the only reason they'd waited so long with their mother's funeral was that they'd hoped their father would return home.

Well, Ward Jackson had come home, and less than 48 hours after seeing him standing in the living room, his casket was being lowered into the ground. The faces around the gravesite were more familiar this time. Ross had deliberately positioned himself next to Mandy. She had not spoken to him, however.

None of the children cried. Silas and Amy were near, but the five Jacksons seemed to huddle together at the edge of the grave. They were still standing in the same position when the service ended and people came over to offer condolences. Mandy and Carrie thanked everyone as they passed by, and when it was down to Silas and Amy, Mandy spoke.

"I didn't know if I'd ever stop wondering where Pa was and how it would be to go back and live with him when he came. I worried at first, but lately I just prayed when I thought of it. Now the wondering is over."

"If you're trying to ask us if you're still welcome in our home, the answer is yes."

"Are you sure? There won't be anyone else coming for us."

"We understand that, and the offer still stands."

"Thank you," Mandy said simply, her eyes still on the grave.

"We'll be at the wagon." Amy spoke the words as she and Silas moved away.

Mandy turned to her siblings. "We can, if you want, go back and live at the house. I could get work in town, and we'd get by somehow."

"Do you want to go back there, Mandy?" Levi asked.

"I want to do whatever everyone else wants, just as long as we're together. Carrie, where do you want to go—out there or with Silas and Amy?"

"With Silas and Amy."

"Levi?"

"Silas and Amy."

"Clovis?"

"Silas and Amy."

"Becca? Becca? Are you going to answer me?"

"What if Pa needs us?"

Mandy hunched down in front of her sister and spoke with her face close. "Becca, Pa won't be home anymore. He's dead, and even if we went back to the house he wouldn't be there. Do you understand?"

"Like Mama."

"Yes, like Mama." They hugged then, and Mandy wondered what was going on in her young mind.

"We're going to stay with you," Becca informed Silas and Amy at the wagon. They accepted this silently, even as their hearts welled up with joy. As the wagon moved in the direction of Grandma Em's, all the children stared in grief at the place that would forever hold the physical bodies of their parents.

— ✢ —

Mandy had determined not to make a fool of herself, as she felt she had done with Ross on their prior meetings. Ross, though unaware of her thoughts, felt her reserve with him even after they'd arrived at Grandma Em's. He hoped it was because of her grief and not something more permanent, as he suspected.

Ross had rejected Mandy, deliberately. Oh, it had been subtle, but it was rejection. Even as he felt a deep sense of loss, he reminded himself that he was the one to blame. She had wanted to get close to him, even before she was saved, but with just enough words and actions, he had carefully kept her at a distance. And now he ached to be close enough to her, emotionally and physically, to allow him the right to comfort her.

But Mandy and Carrie were in deep conversation with Aunt April and as much as he wanted to join them, he didn't feel he had that right.

"How much do lawyers get?" The question interrupted Ross' troubled musings.

"How much do lawyers get for what?" Ross met Levi's direct gaze with friendliness. The boys had come up to stand in front of Ross' chair in the corner of the living room.

"You know, to be a lawyer and catch murderers?"

Ross wasn't prepared for this. His eyes traveled back and forth between the two boys who stood regarding him in open curiosity. They seemed so young to be talking of murder, but Ross knew that when a violent crime was committed it had a way of making one grow up, fast.

"Catching murderers is a job for the sheriff," he explained carefully. "You'd have to talk with him."

Both boys were disappointed with his answer and exchanged a look that said they'd come to a dead end. "We never see the sheriff, and I don't think Silas would take us."

"Have you asked Silas?"

"No. But he's like a pa and pas are funny about what they want kids to do."

And I'm not a pa, Ross thought, *so I was safe to approach.* "I still think it might be a good idea if you ask him," Ross said aloud.

"Does that mean you're going to tell him what we said as soon as we're gone?"

"As a lawyer I'm very good at keeping things confidential." They were clearly at sea with his choice of words, so Ross clarified for them.

"I'll keep my mouth shut."

They moved off then, and he wondered if Silas would thank him for his suggestion. As his attention had not been far from Mandy at the church or Grandma Em's, he knew the exact minute she arose and moved to the kitchen.

37

"Why don't you go out now while you have the chance? Silas and Amy might be ready to leave pretty soon."

"Will you come with me?"

"Sure."

Ross stepped into the kitchen in time to hear this exchange between Mandy and Becca.

"Want to come outside with us, Ross?" Becca had spotted him as they were headed out the door, and Mandy felt like scolding her.

"Maybe Ross is busy, Becca," Mandy said the words softly, honestly hoping he would be.

"I'm not busy," he said easily, even as he wondered why he was pushing himself in where he wasn't wanted. "Where are you headed?"

They were on the porch now, and Becca was yanking her sister by the hand. "Grandma Em said we could pick flowers in the yard. You can help us."

Ross was a few steps behind the forcefully drawn Mandy, and he prayed for the right words to break down the wall he'd erected between them.

Figuring that Mandy would stand and watch Becca pick flowers, he hoped to strike up a conversation with her. No chance. She began picking the delicate blossoms right along with Becca, and Ross hesitated only a moment before he joined them.

Tall and very masculine in his dark suit, Ross looked totally out of place with bunches of wildflowers in his hand. Mandy couldn't stifle a giggle. The laugh caught Becca's attention and she, too, giggled at the awkward-looking Ross.

"I have a funny feeling I'm being laughed at."

"It's just that suits and flowers don't really go together." The words came out hesitantly, and Mandy wished she'd kept her mouth shut; no one wanted to be laughed at.

Ross' brow rose in speculation, his eyes on Mandy, and she felt terrible when he turned back toward the house without a word. But he wasn't leaving as she expected.

Hanging his suit coat on a nail outside the house, Ross rolled up his sleeves. With one hand he scooped up the flowers he'd laid down and rejoined the ladies.

Mandy looked at the way his shoulders and chest filled out his vest and shirt and once again wished she'd kept her mouth shut. Staring for a moment at his muscular forearms, Mandy bent over some flowers hoping he wouldn't notice her fiery cheeks.

"That's a weed, Becca."

"It's still pretty."

"I guess it is at that."

There wasn't much conversation beyond that. Becca praised Ross on some of his selections and he thanked her politely. Mandy noticed how he always treated children with the same respect he accorded adults. Her mind was on Ross instead of where she was picking flowers and seconds later she plunged her hand into a thistle.

Her sharp intake of breath was heard by Ross, and he was at her side in a moment.

"It stings, doesn't it?" He had taken her hand in both of his and turned the palm up for his inspection. Watching the way his thumb moved carefully over her skin, the desire to look up into his face, so close to her own, was nearly overpowering.

"Did you touch a sticker, Mandy?" Becca wanted to know. Mandy was thankful for the opportunity to take her hand back.

"It's fine, really." It did sting, but that was fine with Mandy. Anything to take her mind off Ross, or she'd be looking at him like a lovesick calf again and embarrassing them both.

Becca was picking flowers a ways off and Ross, who had stayed near Mandy, spoke for her ears alone.

"I'm sorry about your dad, Amanda. If there is anything I can do, I hope you'll ask."

"Thank you, Ross. That's kind of you."

"Amanda, will you please look at me when we talk?"

Her hands stilled their movement, but she did not do as she was asked. Ross watched her profile and had to stop his hand from brushing a blade of grass from her cheek.

"No one my own age was ever as nice to me as you've been." The sentence came out of nowhere, but Ross was beginning to understand the way Mandy's thoughts worked. He knew she was about to be brutally honest with him.

"And it's easy for a girl like me who's never had a guy of her own to misunderstand niceness. I know I acted in a way that made you uncomfortable and I'm still embarrassed. That's why I don't look at you when we talk. I'm embarrassed."

"I don't want you to be embarrassed. I want us to be friends." Ross spoke sincerely.

Mandy had to think on that. Ross would be such a nice friend to have. But whether they were friends or not, Mandy was going to be seeing him from time to time with other girls.

"I'd like that," she said simply and finally raised her eyes to his.

Seeing shadows beneath her eyes for the first time, Ross realized how thoughtless it was to talk about his own selfish desire to befriend her when her father had just been killed.

"My timing is always bad, it seems. Here you're grieving for your father and I'm trying to push my friendship on you."

"That's alright. It doesn't feel real to me yet, Pa's death I mean. It's like he was never really here, like I dreamed him coming to the house. And then to be murdered. I don't like to think about that."

"Silas told me the sheriff wants to talk with you tomorrow."

"Yes. I guess I should be thankful. He wanted to talk to me today but Silas told him no."

"Amanda, would you like me to be there when he talks to you? I don't mean to make it sound like you need a lawyer, but if you want me to, I can be there."

"Ross, I appreciate the offer but since you don't really think I would need a lawyer, maybe you'd better not. You see, I can't afford to pay you for your services. But thanks anyhow."

She'd done it again—taken him totally off guard. Just when he thought he was becoming proficient at guessing her thoughts, she said something that took him unawares. It never once occurred to him to charge her for his time, and he told her as much.

"But why wouldn't you?" she wanted to know. "You have to make a living, and you can't do that by giving away your services."

"There would be no charge," he repeated firmly.

"I couldn't do that. That would be taking advantage of our friendship, and even the Bible talks about that."

"It isn't taking advantage of our friendship when I'm offering to help you, Amanda." But she would not be swayed and even though no voices were raised and no emotion showed on Ross' face, he was frustrated with her for not seeing things his way.

The discussion was cut short when Becca needed Mandy. Not long after, they started for home. Ross said nothing when Mandy took her leave, but he would be in the sheriff's office tomorrow when she came to town, whether she wanted him there or not.

38

Mandy stood for a long time with the letter in her hand. It had been such a little thing, Silas' wanting to get the mail on the way home from Grandma Em's. Now Mandy stood in her bedroom with the letter in her hand, not needing to have it opened to know it was from her pa.

"Mandy?"

"Come on in, Carrie. I'm glad you came up. I need someone to pray with me."

Carrie did not need to be asked twice. The girls sat on the bed, and each one petitioned God on behalf of the contents of the letter and any changes it might make in their future.

"I wasn't sure you were going to open the letter; after all, it took you a long time to look at Mama's things. I thought you might want to wait on this, too."

"I'd like to, but it's not the same this time. Pa was murdered and maybe there's something in this letter that will give a clue as to why that happened. With him gone, I wish more than ever that I knew what became of the letter he sent to Mama last winter. I never dreamt it wouldn't be in her papers."

After a few minutes of quiet, Mandy's fingers began to work at the seal on the envelope.

Mandy,

I can't stay here with your ma gone. Cameron is a good man he'll do right by you and the other kids stay with him It was going to be different this time but I can't stay with your ma gone when you miss her think on the good times and the stories around butterfly rock. The rock will help you she

always wanted the best more than we could give.
Tell all of them I care.

Pa

The marked lack of punctuation made some of the sentences unclear. The girls read it over three times and then looked at each other.

"What's butterfly rock?"

"I was just going to ask you that. And the part about the good times and stories."

"There's nothing here . . . you know . . . like I hoped there would be."

"Maybe we should show it to Silas."

But Silas could make no sense of the words. He read the letter to the three younger children but they had no clues.

"I'll mention it to Rufus tomorrow and see what he says. I suspect it was just your father's way of saying good-bye because he was moving on. Mandy, what's bothering you?"

Silas had been watching Mandy's expressive face for a few moments and knew she had something on her mind.

"Well, it's sort of sudden, but after we get done at the sheriff's office I want to go over to the house and gather everything up. Something inside of me needs to have the house cleared out. For some reason it feels like a burden hanging over my head."

"I see no problem with that. I'll give Luke a time and he can meet us over there with a second wagon. We'll take everything you want."

— ✙ —

Mandy was very quiet on the ride into town the next morning, and Silas wondered just how much more she could take. Levi had been impossible at the breakfast table, disrespectful to everyone, and especially Mandy. It was just one more worry on the overburdened heart of this 18-year-old girl. If the dark smudges beneath her eyes were any indication, she was near the breaking point. Silas asked God to sustain her as only He could.

Ross was waiting outside the sheriff's office. Mandy didn't look at all surprised to see him. He held her by the waist to swing her down from the wagon and she gave him a weak smile. His eyes took quick inventory of her fatigued features before he dropped his hands and took her arm to enter the building.

In the space of a few minutes the sheriff told Mandy what she already knew—when, where, and how her father was killed, along with the fact that he had no leads to the murder. They talked about the cryptic letter, and Rufus agreed with Silas that it must have been Ward's way of saying good-bye.

"What about Aaron Marks? You said he was headed out there on business that morning. Did he see anything?" Ross' face was serious.

"I haven't talked to Aaron since he came and told me he'd found Ward. His, uh, housekeeper told me he was going to be away for a few days."

Ross was clearly suspicious and the sheriff gave him a stern look. "Now listen, Ross—I can see what you're thinking and I can't say as I think much of Aaron Marks, but I wouldn't call the man a murderer."

They soon left Rufus' office with Mandy looking utterly drained.

"Maybe we should put off going to the house."

"No, I want to get it over with."

"What's this, something I can help with?" Ross asked and Silas explained the plan. He offered to go with them and the three rode in silence out to the Jackson house.

Luke was on time and the three men made quick work of the beds, table, one dresser, and the handful of chairs. Every time Mandy picked something up one of the men took it from her hands. Finally Ross stepped forward with a small brown book.

"Here's something you can carry. It looks like an old dairy." It was locked and without a key. Not recognizing the book, Mandy could only wonder what was inside the little volume.

"Well, that just about does it. Mandy, why don't you have a look around to see if we've missed something?" Mandy was inside when Luke called from his place by the wagon.

"Looks like we have company." The three men watched two riders approach, and when they drew closer Ross said, "I thought Rufus said Aaron Marks was out of town."

"Well, since Rufus is the man riding with him we'll just ask."

The men had dismounted before anyone spoke, and by then Mandy was back out of the house. Speaking directly to the sheriff, Mandy broke the silence. "I thought you said Mr. Marks was out of town."

"It would seem, Mandy, that his housekeeper was misinformed. The truth is, Mr. Marks just showed me a contract, signed by your father, that states *him* to be the lawful owner of this house and land."

"Easy." Ross' voice, soothing and low, came to Mandy's ears from where he stood just behind her. She tried to relax the muscles that had tensed with this unexpected news.

"Would you have an objection to my seeing the contract?" Ross asked the question, but his direct gaze and professional air made it sound more like an order.

Mandy, standing in front of Ross now, studied his face as he read. His eyes sought hers when he lowered the paper, never leaving them even when he passed the paper to Silas and Luke. He told her the property was legally Marks'.

Had he not had an audience, Ross would have taken Mandy in his arms. He watched her eyes fill with tears and gently brushed her cheek with the backs of his fingers, finding the touch not nearly enough. He turned back to Baxter's sheriff and Aaron Marks, his eyes narrowing in speculation.

"I never met Ward Jackson but I find this a little out of character for all I've heard about the man. He took the risk of leaving his family with *nothing* by not returning by August with gold from your claim? That's an agreement only a fool would sign."

"But sign it he did. Now, if you'll please return it to me I'll be about my business. By the way, did this furniture come from inside the house?"

Silas opened his mouth to protest, content in letting Ross handle matters until now, but Mandy forestalled him. The furniture was all in terrible shape, and there was no fight in her.

"Sheriff, does he have a right to this furniture?"

"I'm afraid so, Mandy." The man looked truly regretful.

"Then we'll unload it." She moved forward and took a chair down which Ross took from her. In no time everything was in a pile outside of the cabin.

"I don't like any of this, Rufus, and I intend to look into the whole thing."

"I don't like it either, Ross, but you can see my hands are tied."

Aaron Marks was inside the cabin and missed the exchange. The men talked for a few minutes more and then Ross stepped to the wagon, where Silas was trying to comfort Mandy.

"I'll be looking into all of this starting tomorrow. In my opinion there are too many things falling nicely into place for Aaron Marks. But for today, I think I should take Amanda in to Grandma Em's. She needs quiet and a place to rest and—"

"Amy might need my help." Mandy's words were ignored, and if she hadn't been so tired she would have resented the way they discussed her as if she weren't there.

"That's fine, Ross," Silas answered when he'd heard him out. "We'll see both of you at supper."

And that, Mandy thought, *was that.* She was lifted into the wagon, and Ross headed the horses toward Grandma Em's.

39

Mandy would not even discuss going up the stairs to one of the bedrooms at Grandma Em's. She took a place on the sofa in the living room, where she could hear the older woman preparing coffee.

Ross came down the stairs with a quilt and a pillow in his arms, and Mandy watched him place them beside her.

"I'm not sleepy, Ross."

"Well you might be before the afternoon is over, and if you won't go to the bedroom I'll bring the bedroom to you."

Mandy's eyes felt like they were filled with sand every time she blinked, making the pillow beside her look inviting after all.

"I'll help Grandma Em with the tray."

Mandy acted as though she didn't hear him, and Ross began to worry about her. He felt guilty about the way he'd insisted she not go home to her family, understanding very well the way her brothers and sisters leaned on her. But the way she unreservedly gave of herself was taxing her to the limit. If she didn't get some rest, she was going to collapse.

"I'm so glad you brought her here, Ross. She's been trying to take care of everyone but herself for too long. Here—you carry the tray in. I want to get my Bible."

Grandma Em was just a few seconds behind Ross in entering the living room. She saw that he'd set the tray down and was trying to carefully remove the quilt from beneath the pillow on which Mandy had fallen asleep.

"Ross," Grandma Em whispered. "Go get the quilt off my bed."

In the time he was gone Grandma Em had lifted Mandy's legs onto the sofa. Ross was able to step forward and gently lay the covering over her.

Mandy stirred then and said without rising, "Is it alright if I sleep here?"

"It's fine, dear. Go back to sleep." Grandma Em was bent over her, and she couldn't see Ross.

"I forgot to thank Ross."

"You'll see him later."

"Okay." The word was said in such a sleepy voice, Grandma Em smiled. Mandy would sleep for a good long time, she was sure of that. Ross carried the tray back to the kitchen where they had their coffee.

— ✣ —

Mandy studied herself in the mirror and then told herself to stop it. "Ross is just a friend."

She shook her head—it wasn't working. She could tell herself that Ross Beckett was just a friend until she was old and gray and it wouldn't change the way her heart quickened when he was near or the way his touch, even accidental, made her feel like she couldn't breathe.

And now he was coming to get her in just a few minutes to head back to Silas and Amy's, and she was primping in front of the mirror as if going to a wedding.

"Oh, your hair is so pretty, Mandy, so dark and thick!"

"It's not as long as I'd like."

Grandma Em had come into the bedroom and sat down in the rocking chair where she could see Mandy in the mirror.

"Oh, but the style is so becoming on you. I didn't even notice the length."

"Thank you." Mandy said the words gratefully and pulled the brush through her hair a few more times.

"Are you looking forward to Ross driving you out?"

Mandy turned and smiled at Grandma Em. "We're just friends." She was careful not to give the wrong impression.

"I understand," Grandma Em said, even as she wondered if Mandy's heart wasn't more involved.

"Thank you for letting me stay this afternoon. I can't believe how long I slept."

"I still think you should have eaten some lunch."

"Amy and Carrie will have supper on, and I'll fill up at home." Grandma Em rose then and even though she was saying something, Mandy wasn't really listening. *I'll fill up at home.* Mandy smiled to herself over her own words. She said a prayer of thanksgiving because the words were true. Silas and Amy's house was her home.

Her next thought was the remembrance of Aaron Marks walking into the cabin as its new owner.

A blind person could see that the house wasn't worth a thing. But it had been home of 18 years, and Mandy was attached to the old shack even though a strong wind could blow it over.

— ✤ —

"All ready to go?" Ross smiled and waited for her to precede him to the wagon. She had never seen him so casual, not that she blamed him for wearing shirtsleeves and light-colored slacks on such a hot day.

"Thanks again, Grandma Em. I'll probably see you Sunday."

"You're welcome, my dear. Oh, before I forget, would you and Carrie think about coming in one weekend in September and helping me with my canning?"

"We'd love to." Mandy was sincerely pleased. She and Carrie loved the fall, and Grandma Em's house was always fun. It also crossed her mind how much closer she'd be to Ross for an entire weekend.

"We'll decide on a date later. You two had better go. Drive carefully, Ross."

She waved them off from the front porch. As they headed down the street, Mandy had a sudden attack of shyness. It was as if Ross had been able to read her thoughts about being near him next month. It was reason enough to be embarrassed in front of him all over again.

"A penny for them."

"What?"

Ross smiled—she'd been a hundred miles away. "A penny for your thoughts."

"They're not worth that much."

"Why don't you let me be the judge of that?"

Oh no, Mandy thought. *What do I say now?* "And if they're private?" she said almost meekly.

"Then I would be the last one to invade that privacy," he assured her kindly. "Let's talk about the weather."

"It's a nice day if it doesn't rain," she said obediently.

Ross laughed. He couldn't help himself. The horse's ears flicked at the sound. "Mandy, you never stop surprising me."

— ✢ —

"Sweetheart, you outdid yourself." Silas pushed his chair back and put a hand over his full stomach.

"Don't forget Carrie and Becca made the pie," Amy reminded her husband.

"Did you really help, Becca?" her oldest sister wanted to know.

"I cut the apples." Becca held up a bandaged finger, and everyone at the table groaned and then laughed.

Coffee was served in the living room and Mandy, after carrying the tray in, saw that the only place left was next to Ross on the sofa. She nearly sat on top of Carrie in an effort to keep from giving him the wrong impression, causing both Carrie and Ross to look at her.

"He doesn't bite, Mandy," Carrie said under her breath, and Ross' chuckle made Mandy's cheeks flame. Amy's chair was far enough away to miss the words, but she looked very pointedly at Ross when she came to hand Mandy her coffee. Her look said, "What have you done to embarrass my girl?"

Ross only smiled back at her as she did her best to look stern. The talk very soon turned to the events of the last few days.

"I haven't got it in for Aaron Marks or anything but a horrendous crime was committed and even if it hadn't been, the whole thing makes me uncomfortable. You don't have any objections to my checking into it, do you, Silas?" asked Ross.

"None at all. Like you said, we didn't know Ward Jackson but it just doesn't seem like something he'd do."

The talk moved on to other topics and then Amy said it was the boys' and Becca's bedtime. Mandy and Carrie did the honors, even though the boys basically took care of themselves. It gave Amy a chance to tease Ross.

"Alright, Ross Beckett, what did you do to make Mandy blush?"

But to her surprise Ross did not laugh. His look was thoughtful and Silas became alert.

"Amy was kidding, Ross."

"I know she was, but I'm not myself where Mandy is concerned and you might as well know it."

"She's been hurt by so many things, Ross, I—" Amy stopped when she saw that Ross understood her.

"I would never deliberately hurt her. You know that. But sometimes, when feelings are unsettled and a person needs time, well, you end up getting hurt just because your most sensitive emotions are involved.

"Then things are all over with you and Sarah?"

"Yes, and I was relieved. That tells you just how *over* they are."

Carrie came into the room then and asked if Ross was going to join them for their evening Bible study. Ross did sit in but as he rode back home on a horse borrowed from the Cameron stables, he couldn't dispel from his mind the sight of Mandy's sweet face when she shared the way God was holding her up during this traumatic time. And then the way she walked him outside when he was ready to leave and thanked him for all he'd done. Once again he had wanted to lay the world at her feet. But tonight there had been a difference. Tonight, for the first time, he'd wanted to kiss Amanda Jackson.

"Oh, Lord," Ross prayed. "I was just telling Amy I wouldn't hurt Amanda and now I'm actually thinking of doing something that would cut her to the quick if I acted on it without loving her."

Ross' heart stayed heavy all the way home and even after he retired. He wondered when his heart had made the change from compassion for Amanda to love and if it really had. And if he did love Amanda, just what was he going to do about it?

40

"What's the problem, boys?" Silas stood in the doorway of Levi and Clovis' room and stared at their stiff backs. They sat side by side on the bed looking out the window, hoping Silas would go away.

He wasn't about to leave the room without an answer, so he came in and sat on his heels in front of them. It brought him down to eye level and they eventually forced their gaze to his.

"Amy called you to breakfast."

"We're sick," Clovis told him.

"You weren't sick last night."

"Well, we're sick today." Levi's chin jutted out aggressively.

"I know you're not happy that this is the first day of school, but you will watch the way you speak to me, Levi Jackson!" Silas watched the fire drain out of the boy.

"I'm sorry." ·

"And I forgive you." It had taken many strong words, revoked privileges, and one severe spanking to get Levi to this point, and Silas knew he couldn't love him more if he was a child of his own body.

"Clovis, are you upset about school?" He would stand by Levi, no matter what, and Silas could see that he wasn't upset.

"I'd rather stay here with you, but I want to learn to read." Silas smiled at the sincerely spoken words.

"We'll talk over breakfast." The words left no argument and Levi filed out the door, his face long. For the first time since being under Silas' roof, Levi wasn't hungry. Not even his parents' death had put him off food. For too many years he'd gone without, but today he did little more than push his breakfast around. Amy watched him with concern, her gaze moving between her husband and Levi.

"Can you tell me, Levi, what you don't like about school?"

"I just don't need to know all that stuff, that's all. I want to raise horses like you, and I don't need to know where China is to do that."

"Well you're right about that; I've never had to go to China. But last month a man underpaid us by fifty dollars. Now you tell me how I would have known that without the math I learned in school.

"Fifty dollars?"

"That's right—it's a lot of money. And since Luke and I share in this business together, both our families would have lost. I know school isn't always fun, but someday you'll have people depending on you. So right now, you do what you need to do to make sure you're worth depending on." Silas hoped the words were on Levi's level. He prayed that they would make a difference in the boy's attitude because Levi was going to school whether he wanted to or not.

"The school is closer here, Levi, that's one nice thing."

For once Levi didn't snap at Carrie and tell her she was dumb. Silas had forbade him to use the word. But Silas' words must have had an effect because Levi was uncharacteristically quiet.

Nothing more was said about school. Amy felt a little bereft as she kissed the three middle children and watched them walk away from the house. Becca would not be six for another few days and with all that had happened during the summer, Silas and Amy had decided to keep her home for another year.

Amy watched the children until they were out of sight. Carrie wore a new dress of pale blue trimmed in white, and the boys had on navy slacks with navy and white plaid shirts. She wondered what they would look like at the end of the day.

Silas watched Amy turn suddenly from the front door and retreat behind the closed door of the bedroom. Mandy offered to go out to the swings with Becca. Silas followed his wife.

"I'm an ingrate, Silas, the biggest there is. God has given us these five wonderful children and still I want more."

"There's nothing wrong with you still desiring a baby of your own, Amy." Another month had come, she'd told him that morning, and though it was easier with the children here, it didn't diminish the ache inside to conceive and bear life on her own.

"I'm afraid the children will suspect how I feel. I can't stand the thought that they would think they're not enough. I do love them with all my heart and praise God for them everyday."

"They're not going to think that. They know how you love them. Every Christian has hurts and this is one of yours, but you go to God every time and He holds you."

"I keep thinking about what Mandy shared, you know, about all her mother's pregnancies. I hurt because I can't get pregnant, Si, but it's nothing compared to having eight babies and having to bury three of them."

"I know, sweetheart. I know." Silas' arms were around her in a tender embrace. He'd felt the same way when Mandy had shared during Bible study one night. She and Carrie had been rather accepting of the whole thing, but the news was horrible to Amy. The fact that she was a woman made it more real for her than for Silas, along with her fatigue from the pace of being a mother to five.

"I've been thinking about us getting away for a few days. Gram wants Carrie and Mandy to come in this month and help her with the canning. I know Mac and Julia would take the boys, and I'm sure Mark and Sue would love to have Becca. It would just be a few days, over a weekend, but I think we both need it."

"Oh, Silas, do you really think we could? I mean, you don't think the kids will feel deserted?"

"Nope. The boys will have Cal and Charlie to fight and play with, and Becca has never seen as many dolls as

Mark's girls have. Carrie and Mandy were already going to stay with Gram. It's perfect."

Amy threw her arms around her husband's neck and squeezed him. "I think you're wonderful, Silas Cameron."

41

"Thank you, Grandma Em." Mandy spoke the words quietly as she took her place in church. On her way down the aisle, Grandma Em had reached out and given her the diary she left at her house the day she stayed there to rest.

She fingered the small volume lightly and almost wished they were headed home instead of to Grandma Em's so she could ask Silas to open it for her right away. But then her eye caught the movement of Ross and Pete coming in to take a pew, and the hope that Ross would be at Grandma Em's for dinner was enough to make her want to stay in town.

The congregation stood for a few songs and then Pastor Chad introduced a special musical number.

"Most of you probably remember last Easter when Amy wrote and sang a song for us. Even though it's an Easter song, I asked Amy to sing it again. She calls it, 'Song for the Other Mary.'"

Silas took his seat behind the piano and in a few moments the church was filled with the sound of Amy's beautiful voice singing 'Song for the Other Mary....'

"Thank you, Silas and Amy, for those words taken directly from this morning's passage. Let's open our Bibles to the book of Matthew, chapter 28.

"It's taken us a long time to get to this final chapter, with a guest speaker one week and me sick another. I also wanted to move slowly; in fact we probably won't get through this chapter today.

"Last time I spoke about the cave where they laid Jesus' body, covering the entrance with a huge stone. Now Jesus Himself foretold of His rising again on the third day and this worried the chief priests and the Pharisees. When they brought their concern to Pilate he told them to post a guard for three days, put a seal on the stone, and make it as

Song for the Other Mary

Words by Lori Wick

Music by Timothy Barsness

secure as they could. They feared the disciples would come and steal Christ's body to make it look like He'd risen from the dead.

"How blind they were to think that Jesus' body would need to be smuggled out in the night. As if that stone, no matter how tremendous in size, or those soldiers could actually hold the Son of God when He rose from the dead. But of course in their unbelief they had no comprehension of God's power.

"Now in chapter 28, it's dawn. Some women, the Bible says Mary Magdalene and the other Mary, came to look at the grave. When they got there they found that a great earthquake had occurred. An angel sent from God came and rolled the stone away and sat on it. The Bible says he looked like lightning, and was as white as snow, and all the soldiers fell down as if they were dead.

"Try to picture this scene: The huge rock is rolled away, the entrance to the tomb is showing, and all the men they put to guard the grave are lying on the ground. On the top of this rock sits an angel.

"You can imagine how surprised the ladies were when the angel spoke to them. He said, "Fear not," which tells us they were probably terrified; I'm sure I would have been. And the angel leads them in and shows them that the body is not there. Christ had risen just like He said He would.

"The angel tells the women to spread the news. He also says that they will see Christ later. Verse 8 says they ran with fear and great joy to tell the disciples. Whom should they meet on the way—none other than Jesus Christ! The Word says they fell down at his feet and worshiped Him.

"Beloved, will you have a chance to fall down and worship at Christ's feet? Have you ever faced eternity and believed that Christ died and rose again for you? Because if you haven't, then you can't plan on seeing the Lord, you can't plan on living with Him for forever, as these women did.

"Recently I had the privilege of leading a young woman to the Lord. She is only 15 years old. Now you might say to me, what kind of sins can a 15-year-old commit—but she knew she needed a Savior. And I think you do, too. It's so simple. Tell God you sin and need a Savior. He's waiting to take you into His arms."

Pastor Nolan closed then with a prayer that no one would leave the room unless they were sure of where they'd spend eternity. He also announced before he prayed that he would be down front if anyone wanted to come and talk with him about salvation.

During the prayer Carrie felt Mandy's eyes on her. She looked beside her to see her sister's very wet smile. Carrie's heart overflowed and so did her eyes. They hugged as soon as the prayer was over.

"Two of us down and three to go, Carrie," Mandy whispered in her ear. "It's just a matter of time." Carrie couldn't answer, so tight was her throat. They clung to each other for a few seconds longer, each praying that she would be sharing heaven with her siblings.

42

Later at Grandma Em's, Mandy looked across the table at Charles as he told about the first few days of school.

"The most fun is watching Cal go up front and stand next to Miss Franks. He's about three feet taller than she is."

"Charlie, she's not that short," Cal said with a good-natured grin. He took in stride the fact that he was probably going to be as enormous as his father.

"She's not much bigger than Robyn, Cal, and you know it."

Calvin laughed at the image of his teacher being the same size as his four-year-old sister. It was just the reaction Charlie wanted. He was the character at the MacDonald house, with the ability to make people laugh in every situation. His grin was downright infectious.

"I hope you boys are not being disrespectful. Miss Franks came very highly recommended," their father remarked.

"Well, that's the only thing that is high about her 'cause she looks like a stiff breeze could carry her away."

"Charles," Mac reprimanded him.

Mandy had to bite her lower lip, she found Charlie's description so amusing. She picked up her glass and her sparkling eyes met those of Ross, framed by the doorway where he was seated at the dining room table. Mandy watched as one eyebrow winged its ways upward and she had the distinct impression he'd been watching her. The thought made her face heat.

"I'll bet it's quiet around the house these days, Mandy," Julia said as she passed her the squash.

"Becca says there's no one to play with. I offer, and she tells me I'm too big. About the only thing she wants my company for is to push her on the swing."

"I'll have to come get her one of these days to play with Robyn. We're looking forward to having Levi and Clovis next weekend. Are you excited to be staying with Gram?"

"We've never lived in town before. I can't wait," Carrie enthusiastically answered for both girls. Julia smiled. She hoped that Robyn would be half as sweet as either of these girls when she got to be their ages.

Both Mandy and Carrie stayed out of the kitchen during cleanup because there were plenty of hands. Mandy was at the bottom of the stairway when Rachael's cry sounded from upstairs. Knowing Christine was in the kitchen, she went up to get the baby.

"Rachael Amanda," she crooned in a singsong voice. "Mama is busy and you're not going to starve." The words had no affect on the screaming infant, but Mandy wasn't the least bit intimidated by tears and patiently stood in the bedroom and continued to reason with her cousin.

"Are you pinching her?"

"No," Mandy smiled at Ross. "This is a mad cry because no one is feeding her."

"Give her to me." Mandy's look spoke volumes of skepticism, but Ross ignored her and took Rachael into his arms. To Mandy's amazement she stopped crying. Ross looked so smug, she chuckled.

"I can see you're very proud of yourself."

"It just takes a man's touch."

Mandy shook her head. "You'd better enjoy it while it lasts, because she's hungry and watching you is only going to distract her just so long."

As if on cue, Rachael's features screwed up again and nothing Ross did could quiet her. Christine arrived shortly afterward, with Kate on her heels, to feed her infant daughter.

"How have you been?" Ross asked Mandy as they walked down the stairs.

"I've been fine. How about you?"

"I'm fine. I've done some checking like I said I would, and I'm not coming up with anything very remarkable. I'd like to go back out to the house but that would be considered trespassing, and asking for permission from Aaron Marks would be a waste of breath."

"It's not that important right now, since we live with Amy and Silas. But some day, when Levi and Clovis are older, it would have been nice to know they had a little bit of land they would call their own, to live on or sell if they needed the money. We even had a buyer."

"Someone wanted to buy your land?" The attorney in Ross became very alert.

"The man who owns the adjoining land. His name is Mr. Brooks. He lives in Reedsburg, but he plans to move to Baxter when his children are grown. He loves the bluffs and rocks out our way and gave Pa some money a long time ago to give him first option if we ever wanted to sell. But it's not our decision now. When Mr. Brooks builds on his land, his neighbor will be Aaron Marks."

"Did your father and Mr. Brooks agree to this on paper? Did your father sign something, like a contract or an agreement?"

"Yes, I think it was all legal. There's a paper in with Mama's things that explains it all."

"Could I see the paper soon?"

Mandy's eyes widened. "You think there might be something on the paper?"

"I don't want to get your hopes up but it would be very nice if we could get a judge to say that the first agreement cancels the one with Aaron Marks."

"Ross I never thought of that."

"Well, I'm not sure it's possible but it's worth checking into."

"Maybe Silas is coming into town this week and he could bring it. If not, they'll be bringing me in on Thursday evening to stay here with Grandma Em and I could bring it then."

"That's fine." Ross agreed with the plan, even as his hopes grew. He knew himself well enough that he would never be able to wait until Friday to get that paper. He thought of when he could ride out to get it and then he realized what Mandy had said, that this coming weekend was when she and Carrie were coming into town to stay.

"Why are you grinning at me, Ross?" His look had gone from business to something far more personal, and Mandy knew she was going to blush if he continued to stare at her.

"Can't I smile at you, Amanda?"

She took refuge in a question she'd been wanting to ask him. "Why do you always call me Amanda?"

"Don't you like your name?"

"It's not that I don't like it—it's just that everyone calls me Mandy but you."

They had walked out the front door as they talked and were headed for the backyard. Ross stopped her for a moment at the side of the house so they could be alone. He hesitated and then was as honest with her as she always was with him. "I think of the name Mandy as a nickname for a little girl and I do not, in any way, Amanda, think of you as a little girl."

The low tone in his voice made her feel as if he were embracing her. She stood very still, wanting to take her statement back and trying not to read anything into the look Ross was giving her. She knew she couldn't take another rejection. It would be better to never talk with Ross again than to get close and be pushed away.

"I need to check on the boys." Mandy started away, but Ross caught her hand. She spoke without looking at him.

"I can't take a chance, Ross, that I'm imagining what I see or that you'll change your mind."

"Amanda, you're not—"

"Please let go, Ross," she interrupted him. He did so, reluctantly. The pleading tone in her voice had been too much.

As Ross watched her walk away, it was his turn to plead. "Heavenly Father, show me, help me. She's so precious and vulnerable, and I can't get her out of my mind. But please, God, please don't let me hurt her."

43

"Thanks, sweetheart. Okay, Mandy, try this key from Amy's diary." Silas took the tiny key from his wife's hand and handed it to his oldest adopted daughter. The whole family watched as she put the key into the lock and worked it gently.

"Let me try." Silas took the diary and, after a few seconds of rattling and twisting, the small lock sprang open. Silas handed the book back to Mandy, and everyone crowded around to see her open it.

"I can't see," Becca complained and Silas swung her up into his arms.

"The first entry is in May, just after I was born!" Mandy exclaimed.

No one thought to get comfortable in the living room. They huddled in the space outside of Silas and Amy's bedroom, looking over Mandy's shoulder as she read several pages. Some entries were months apart and not every word was legible. But all were dated and the children were given a last glimpse, a last touch, from their mother.

When Mandy could no longer see the pages through her tears, she handed the book to Carrie. But Carrie was in the same state, and within the space of a few seconds all of the children were crying. Silas looked on helplessly, as even his wife's tears fell, before going to the piano and playing very softly the song Amy had sung in church.

It took some time but eventually they were all gathered around the piano and Amy sang. Mandy and Carrie were still very emotional and their tears would not stop. Levi, Clovis, and Becca had stopped crying and were stationed as close to Silas' moving hands as they could be. When he stopped playing, Clovis spoke. "Can you teach me to do that?"

"To play the piano?"

"Yeah."

"Anytime, son."

"Am I really your son?" Silas sat frozen for an instant. The quiet, well-behaved, seemingly *need* less Clovis was looking as if his very life depended on Silas' answer.

"I would never do anything to make you forget your mother and father, but Clovis, I think of you as my son. I think of all of you as my own children. It doesn't matter that Amy and I are not your physical parents, you're *ours*."

Silas lifted Clovis into his lap and held him close. He reached for Levi next and cuddled the boy to his chest. Silas' tears came when, for the first time, Levi hugged him back. His face was still wet as he put his arms around Becca. Mandy and Carrie, who had just stopped crying, were again sobbing when Silas came to embrace them.

There were no arguments about an early bedtime; everyone was drained. Amy lay dozing, comforted to feel the mattress beneath her back.

"I'm amazed, Silas, at how comfortable and responsive the children are and after such a short period of time."

"It's got to be the Lord."

"I can understand why they go to you because their need for a father was so desperate, but *me*, Silas? I just can't understand how loving they are to me." After Silas had hugged them, the children had gone of their own accord to Amy and embraced her without a trace of reserve.

"I don't think it's hard to understand. A child couldn't help but react in turn to the love and kindness you show."

"Mandy's not a child." Silas said nothing in answer to Amy's serious comment.

Both of them had been in the backyard when Mandy had come around the corner of the house, face flushed and looking miserable. Her very stance said she did not want to be questioned. Things became even more confusing when Ross, looking equally upset, followed her and watched her from a distance until it was time to go home.

"We've got to remember what Ross said to us the night he came to supper—that he wouldn't hurt her."

"That might not be as easy as he thinks. When one person's feelings have gone deeper than another's . . ." Amy did not go on. The words were too painfully close to the hard start she and Silas had shared.

"God loves Mandy and He knows very well how bruised she is right now. We've got to trust that He will take care of her, sweetheart. This isn't like when Becca falls and needs a kiss—I wish it were. This is much more serious. We've prayed about spouses for the girls, and I have to believe that God loves them enough to give them the best."

These were comforting words on which to fall asleep, words that Mandy could have used as she slowly turned the pages of the diary and read in bed by lamplight.

She could almost see the change in her mother as she turned the pages. Carefree and in love, raising a little girl. Then maturing into a woman who wonders where her husband is and how she'll ever get over having to bury one of her babies. As the picture on the dresser faded into the woman Mandy grew up with, she knew she had to put the book down.

She tried to pray in the darkness then, wanting to thank God that He'd saved her and to praise Him for His love. Other nights she would have gone on to ask God to save Levi, Clovis, and Becca. She would also have asked for wisdom and a daily thirst for the Word, but tonight her mind could only conjure up one image and that was the face of Ross Beckett.

"I love you, Ross." The words were said into her pillow as sleep came over her. She wished it were Ross' ears hearing them.

— ❖ —

"Your deal, Aaron."

"Aaron, are you in the game?"

Aaron Marks took up the cards without comment and began to deal. The hope that a card game would divert his thoughts hadn't worked. He was losing money hand over fist and his mood was growing blacker by the second.

Something was not quite right, he was sure. There was some loose end that was going to trip him up, and until he found out what it was he would not rest.

A sudden memory of Mandy Jackson standing in front of the shack came to mind. She was holding a small book. He'd bet plenty it was something she'd taken from inside. He played around with the idea of having the sheriff go after it but quickly ruled it out. The man was a bleeding heart and could not be bought. In Marks' estimation that made him worthless.

No, he'd have to get his hands on the book himself. He could use another look at those papers too. Last time he'd been in too much of a hurry and only took the letter. His attention suddenly turned back to the game, and he won the hand.

He had a course of action now, he thought with a smile, and everything would be fine.

44

"When do you expect the girls?" Preston asked as he took another sip of coffee.

"This evening. Si and Amy are taking a late train for Neillsville. Amy said they would spend tomorrow with her dad before heading off on their own."

"Will Carrie go to school tomorrow?"

"She'll walk with Mark's girls. Then Mandy and I will go to work. I know Carrie will want to stay away from school since it's the end of the week, but I don't feel right about that."

"When will Silas and Amy be back?"

"Monday night, or maybe afternoon. Cora spoils you, Preston. This lunch was wonderful." The words were deliberately spoken as Preston's ancient-looking housekeeper and cook came in to serve dessert. In exchange for her compliment, Emily was given a toothless grin before the old woman shuffled out of the room.

"She's one of a kind—I'll give her that. I can't think what would happen to her if I didn't need her anymore." The words lay between them, feeling like a rushing river, frightening to cross.

"I'm an old woman, Preston, set in my ways." Emily spoke quietly, honestly.

"And I wouldn't change a thing about you." The expression on his face made the words a promise.

"I believe you wouldn't. What I can't believe is that you don't want someone young, someone who could give you years of companionship."

"I believe we would have years together, but if it was only six months Emily, it would be worth every second."

She slid her hand along the table top then, and Preston's fingers closed over hers. "Will you join the girls and me for supper on Saturday night?"

"I'd love to," he said with a smile.

"Why don't you bring Peter and Ross."

"Peter plans to go to Reedsburg for the weekend to see his folks, but I'll ask Ross."

"Something tells me he'll jump at the chance."

— ⁝ —

"How's my little Robyn bird?" Silas swung his niece up into his arms and nuzzled her neck. She giggled, looking down at Levi and Clovis.

"You're sleepin' in my room and I'm sleepin' in with Mama."

"Hi, boys," Mac came out of the house toward the wagon. He lifted a small traveling bag from the back, and told the boys they had about half an hour before supper.

Levi and Clovis started off with Charlie. Silas put Robyn down and grabbed them to him.

"Have fun, and I'll see you sometime Monday."

"Do we walk home with Charlie or go to our house?"

"Come here to Mac's." He hugged and kissed each one and then sent them off with a gentle tap to their backsides.

Mac and Silas watched as the three boys disappeared around the corner of the house with Robyn in hot pursuit.

"I don't think there will be any trouble, but you do what you have to, Mac."

"I'm sure we'll be fine." Mac laughed as Silas stood gripped with indecision. "Si, they're going to be fine. Julia and I have a *little* experience with boys, and we'll handle whatever comes up."

Thanking his brother-in-law, Silas headed for home to get all his girls before heading to town. They were ready so the wagon was loaded swiftly. Amy laughed at Becca, who was unable to sit still on the seat in her enthusiasm.

Susanne was treated to the same look Mac had seen as Becca barely took time to be hugged good-bye. Silas stared after her skipping feet and flying pigtails, bereft.

194

"It's pretty hard to lose out to cousins and dolls, isn't it, Silas?" Sue's soft words were spoken in kindness, not teasing.

"I guess I think they're not going to survive the weekend without us. But we do need to get away, and once we're on the train I'll be fine."

"Don't forget that if something comes up we can go for Mandy."

"Thanks, Sue." Silas was grateful for her words. In the next minute he was back in the wagon where Amy and the older girls waited. Then they were on their way to his grandmother's.

"Have a good time," she told them.

"Thanks Gram, we'll be back sometime Monday."

"If for some reason you're held up, we'll be just fine."

"Well, girls," Grandma Em spoke as they watched Silas and Amy walk toward the train station, "I've got supper started. Why don't you take your things up and pick out bedrooms?"

"Can we stay in that green room I was in the other day?"

"That's fine, Mandy. That was Christine's room when she lived with me, before she and Luke were married. Carrie, you can take the other room if you like. There's a crib in there but it's still comfortable."

"I'll sleep in with Mandy. We have separate rooms at home, and I kind of miss our talks at night."

"You never told me that, Carrie," Mandy said as they started inside. "You know you can come in anytime."

Grandma Em, with a smile on her face, listened to them talk their way up the stairs. This was going to be a fun weekend.

The three of them had just finished the dishes when Ross knocked at the door. His plans to get out to Silas' sometime that week had fallen through. He hoped Amanda had brought the papers.

"Hi, Ross," Carrie answered the door and opened it wide for him to enter.

"Hi, Carrie. Is Amanda here?"

"She's in the kitchen."

"Who is it, Carrie? Oh, Ross, come in." Grandma Em came from the direction of the kitchen. "We've just finished eating, but I can fix you a plate if you're hungry."

"No, thank you, I've eaten. Amanda was supposed to bring me a document from her mother's papers."

"She's in the kitchen. Why don't you go in and ask her?"

45

Mandy's stomach had begun to churn at the sound of Ross' voice and became downright queasy as he headed into the kitchen.

She had not forgotten the papers he had asked to see, but she *had* forgotten that she told him she would be here Thursday night. Mentally she was preparing herself for seeing him on Sunday, and now he was headed her way. She looked around the pantry where she stood and wished she could just shut the door and have him go away.

"Hello."

"Hi, Ross," she spoke casually as she turned away from the shelf and wondered how her voice could sound so normal. "Are you here about the papers?"

Superficially, yes, he wanted to say. *But the real reason I'm here is because knowing you were so close made it impossible to stay away.*

Aloud he said, "Did you remember them?"

"They're upstairs. I'll run and get them."

But Ross did not step out of her way, and Mandy couldn't stop her eyes from meeting his. It was a mistake.

"I had a busy week, but you were never far from my thoughts."

Mandy wordlessly shook her head, as though trying to deny his words.

"You can't run from me forever, Amanda. We need to talk."

"I don't think I can."

Ross felt defeat wash over him as her eyes filled with tears.

"Please don't cry, Amanda."

"I can't help it, and if you don't want to watch you'd better leave!"

It was the first time she had ever sounded the least bit cross with him, and he realized how selfish it was to ask someone not to cry. It was as if he were saying, "Your tears distress me and *I* don't want to be troubled by them."

Ross closed the small space between them and took her into his arms. Mandy tipped her head back to look up at him, and Ross bent his.

"Mandy?" It was Carrie's voice, from a discreet distance away from the doorway. It stopped Ross cold. "Are you okay, Mandy?"

Ross released her and Mandy took a step back. Her voice shook as she spoke, but what she was thinking had to be said.

"We can be friends, Ross, at least I hope we can, but *do not* touch me again unless you're ready to make up your mind. My heart can't take it."

"What makes you think I haven't made up my mind?"

She looked him square in the eye as she answered. "A man in love would have kissed me just now. You were relieved that Carrie interrupted us—I could feel it in the way your arms relaxed. A man in love would have wanted that kiss as much as I did. Any privacy, no matter how scant, would have been enough to continue." She pushed her way past him, saying as she did, that she would bring him the papers.

— ✥ —

You were relieved that Carrie interrupted us.

Ross set the bundle of papers aside. How excited he had been at the prospect of finding some loophole in Marks' document, but now that he had everything laid out, he couldn't concentrate on a single word.

Amanda had said she did not have time to sort through the papers, so she'd brought the whole bundle. Ross had come across old news clippings and a few letters, all from Amanda's father to her mother. The document was there, signed just as Amanda said it was, but Ross was too emotionally worn to do any research.

He'd been wrong to hold her. He knew that now. And she was right—he hadn't made up his mind. There was something missing, something that was holding him back. With Sarah it had all felt so right, but there hadn't been the heartstopping, breathless reaction to just being near each other that there was with Amanda.

It didn't feel so right and comfortable with Amanda. When he was with her he felt as if his world was out of kilter. And when he wasn't with her he felt like part of him was missing.

Maybe he was really supposed to talk to her about Christ and nothing more. Ross set the papers on his bedside table and blew out the lamp. Things were going to be quiet when Pete left for the weekend. Ross usually fell asleep to the sound of his snoring coming through the wall, as it was now.

"Don't ever forget, Ross, God is the creator of love and marriage." These had been Grandma Em's words when he was in a quandary over Sarah. "You must consult with Him about your future mate because He already has someone picked out for you."

Ross, feeling drained of spirit and will, slid out of bed and to his knees on the floor. His burden was lifted as he gave Amanda to God as well as any future plans God had for him, with or without her. When he finally climbed back between the sheets, he fell asleep trusting that God was in control and that His infinite love for both him and Amanda would guide and shield them in the days to come.

"Luke, what is it?"

"I thought I heard something."

"At the barn?"

"No, toward Si's."

Husband and wife stood at the open bedroom window and looked across at the empty house. The oaks that gave privacy to Silas and Amy's house had lost most of their leaves, giving a clearer view of the two-story structure, but also allowing the moon to cast eerie shadows on the white paint.

"I guess it was just the wind. I'll go over and check on things in the morning."

They went back to bed then, and when a horse and rider eventually moved slowly away from the shadows of the oaks, Luke and Christine were sleeping too soundly to hear.

46

It was late in the afternoon on Saturday and Grandma Em, Mandy, and Carrie had been hard at work for hours. Grandma Em couldn't stop thanking the girls, telling them repeatedly how long it would have taken her to do the fall canning alone.

Mandy lifted the lid on a pot of boiling apples. The steam dampened her hair and put even more color in her already flushed cheeks.

"Okay, Carrie, I'm ready for the jars."

"Is this the last of it?"

"Yep."

Not much later, Preston was at the door with three bouquets of flowers.

"Thank you," Carrie breathed in awe. "Aren't they pretty, Mandy?"

"They're beautiful. Thank you, Mr. Culver."

"You're welcome, ladies."

The girls took their flowers to the kitchen for water, and Preston looked at Emily, who had remained silent. Her smile nearly stretched off her face, and her eyes thanked him in a way that made words unnecessary.

"I take it I did the right thing?"

"You did the right thing."

"Good." He smiled back at her. She reached for his arm as they walked back to the kitchen.

"If the smell in here is any indication, you ladies are very good cooks."

"Hello," Ross called from the porch, and very shortly all five of them were gathered around the kitchen table enjoying chicken and dumplings.

Conversation was light and if Ross and Mandy were not as comfortable as they once would have been, it did not dampen anyone's spirits or detract from the delicious meal.

Coffee was served on the front porch as a lovely breeze blew away any remaining mosquitoes. Grandma Em and Preston had the younger people laughing with stories from their days as kids.

"We were such rascals," Preston began as the evening neared an end. "I remember when I was about ten we decided to put a snake in the teacher's desk. Well, I was the idea man, and none of the other boys ever seemed to notice that I came up with the plans but never got my hands dirty, so to speak.

"Well, I was the delegator on this job and for a very good reason: I'm scared to death of snakes, always have been. Well, I instructed a particular boy to find the snake, and set the time everyone was to meet at the schoolhouse. Then under the guise of watching for the teacher, I stayed well away from the actual snake handling.

"It was 'long about mid-morning and I guess we weren't very bright, because it never occurred to us that the snake could get out of the desk. The teacher had opened her desk several times and still there was no scream.

"I remember it was right in the middle of spelling. Faith Lambert, the best speller in class, was up front, and I looked down to find our snake curled up, calm as you please, right next to my foot.

"I came out of my chair as though my pants were on fire and nearly jumped into the lap of the kid in the next desk. It didn't take long for the teacher to catch on for whom the snake was meant, and she knew who the instigator had been. At the time, I didn't recognize the look, but I realize now what a terrible time she had keeping a straight face when she said there would be no punishment because she was sure I'd learned my lesson. I thought the other guys would never let me live it down."

Everyone had tears of laughter on their faces as they

pictured the dignified Preston Culver jumping through the air in fear of a snake.

"You wouldn't get along very well with Levi, Mr. Culver," Mandy told him. "He loves snakes. The last one he found he named Henry and wanted to keep it in the house. I thought Amy was going to faint."

"And I thought Silas would be in a heap of trouble," Carrie added. "He laughed about the whole thing after the boys went outside. Amy wasn't very happy with him. She made Mandy check the boys' pockets for days after that."

The evening was a great success, and the girls went up to bed tired but content. Mandy had resigned herself to the fact that there would be no future for her and Ross. And with that knowledge, she prayed constantly about getting over him. The evening had gone better than she'd hoped. He had been kind without being too personal. He'd obviously come to the same conclusion as she.

At first she was sorry he was coming to supper but then the practical side of her emerged and she knew she'd be seeing him at family functions for a long time. There was no use in putting off the inevitable.

"Mandy, I forgot to tell you—I'm sorry if I interrupted anything Thursday night between you and Ross."

"Don't apologize, Carrie, You did interrupt, but it was for the best."

"Did he kiss you?"

"Almost."

Mandy's impressionable sister absorbed this in silence.

"Is it wrong to kiss before you're married?"

"I don't know," Mandy answered honestly. "I don't think it's a good idea if you're not committed to each other."

"And you don't think you and Ross will be committed in some way?"

"I thought for a time we might be, but my feelings are stronger than his, and every time I turn around I get hurt. Maybe I'm expecting too much. We can't always control our hearts, and there isn't much I can do about the fact that Ross doesn't share my feelings."

"I'll pray for you, Mandy."

"Thanks, Carrie."

"Uh, Mandy, did Mr. Culver say Pete was coming back tomorrow?"

Mandy turned and stared at her sister in the lamplight. Carrie's voice had been almost strained in an effort to make the question sound casual.

"Carrie, is there something you want to tell me?"

Carrie only looked back at Mandy and bit her lower lip. Mandy went over and sank down on the edge of the full-size bed where Carrie was already beneath the covers.

"It's awful, isn't it?"

"Yeah," Carrie agreed.

"I've fallen for someone who doesn't feel the same. And you like someone who's too old for you."

"He's only 22, same age as Ross."

"And you just turned 15, Carrie." Mandy's words were muffled by the nightgown she was slipping over her nead, but the logical tone in her voice came through loud and clear.

When she emerged, she heard Carrie sigh. Mandy blew out the lamp and crawled into bed beside her. Carrie's voice was a little frustrated when she spoke.

"You're too practical, Mandy. To hear you talk, you're not bothered or hurt by any of this."

"I hurt, Carrie, believe me. I hurt."

47

"Carrie, it's wrong!"

"Well I'm not the least bit tired, and we'd be back and she wouldn't even miss us."

It was Sunday evening and the girls were having a whispered argument on the front porch. Grandma Em had claimed exhaustion and taken herself off to bed. Carrie, Mandy noticed, had energy to spare and was actually entertaining the idea of going for a walk at dusk without asking Grandma Em.

"You don't have to come, Mandy."

"I've a good mind to march right up those stairs and tell Grandma Em what you're thinking of doing."

"And she'd probably give me permission to go. I'm not a little girl, Mandy."

Mandy threw up her hands in exasperation when she saw Carrie was determined.

"Mandy, I'm glad we came in to stay with Grandma Em, and I'm glad that Silas and Amy were able to take a trip. But the whole family stayed so long today. I don't feel like I've been able to do anything fun here in town. I go to school tomorrow and then we go home." She walked down the steps and turned back to look up at her sister.

"I'll be back before dark. If it makes you feel better, you can wait here on the porch."

It took Mandy a moment to see that she was really going. She glanced back at the front door and then moved down the steps to catch up with Carrie.

— ❖ —

"How are your folks?" Ross asked Pete.

"They're fine. My sister is now engaged, but they're waiting until next summer to get married."

"Next summer? Why so long?"

"I don't know. I'd tell her no if I was Donald."

"You and me both. The whole courting process is too painful to wait for the wedding *once* you've actually decided to take the step."

"Yeah, that's the way I feel. Why are we sitting out here on the porch? It's getting dark and cold."

"No good sense, I guess."

"Who is that coming down the street?" Pete said then.

"It looks like Amanda and Carrie, but I can't believe it would be."

— ❖ —

"Carrie Jackson!" Mandy said furiously. "I can't believe you're taking us right past Ross and Peter's. You ought to be ashamed of yourself. We're turning back right now. It's almost dark."

"Too late." Mandy was too angry to notice that Carrie sounded regretful. Halting, the sisters watched as the men approached.

Ross had to stop himself from asking if Grandma Em knew where they were. They weren't little girls and the hour wasn't exactly late, but it was nearly dark and he had a sneaking suspicion Grandma Em was completely unaware of their whereabouts.

"What brings you ladies out this evening?" Pete asked casually, even as his own mind swarmed with questions.

Mandy wanted to pinch Carrie for getting them into this and then standing there as if she had no tongue.

"We're just out for a walk. In fact we were just headed back, weren't we, Carrie?"

"How was your weekend, Pete?" Carrie completely ignored Mandy's question, and even when Mandy pulled on her arm, she did nothing more than stare at Pete.

"I had a nice time, Carrie, thank you. How are things with Grandma Em?"

"Fine."

"Did you get your canning done?"

"Yes."

There was a painful silence then, at least it was painful to Mandy, but she couldn't help but notice how kind Pete was to Carrie. He didn't treat her like she was some kid beneath his notice but talked to her in open friendliness.

"We really have to be going now." Mandy gave Carrie no choice this time but pulled her around until they were headed back down the street.

"We'll walk with you."

"No!" Mandy nearly shouted at Ross. She took a breath to try and calm herself. "Thank you, Ross, but we'll get ourselves home."

Holding Carrie's arm in a grip that would probably leave bruises, Mandy led her away from the men. Peter and Ross exchanged one very brief look before starting after them at an unhurried pace.

They made no effort to hide their intentions to follow but kept a discreet distance between them. Every once in a while Mandy's voice was heard rebuking Carrie. About halfway to Grandma Em's Mandy figured their protectors were not going to go back, so she and Carrie came to a stop and let them catch up.

Pete walked in front with Carrie beside him, and Ross brought up the rear with a steaming Amanda at his side.

"I take it this little walk was not your idea?"

"No, it wasn't! I have no desire to come around where I'm not wanted!" She was just angry enough, her pride smarting at the appearance of coming to see Ross, to throw caution to the wind and say exactly what was on her mind.

"Amanda, did you ever think that the way things are between us hurts me, too?"

Not knowing what to say, Mandy didn't answer. In all of her pain she hadn't considered that Ross might be suffering as well.

They were at the house now, and Carrie's hand flew to her mouth when she looked up to see Grandma Em on the porch. She was thankful for the darkness because she could feel her cheeks burning with shame.

"Are you girls alright?"

The words were said in such anxiety that Carrie burst into tears. "Come on in, girls. You boys come in, too."

After many tears, apologies, and hugs, everyone found themselves in the kitchen with cheese and apples, waiting for hot cocoa. Grandma Em spoke in understanding.

"You finally get a weekend in town and all you do is work. I'm not saying what you did was right, but I think I understand and wish you'd come to me. Now, no more apologies," Grandma Em stopped Carrie from speaking. "It's over and I'll even leave it up to you to tell Silas and Amy."

The girls exchanged a glance, and Mandy knew that Carrie herself felt she should do the unpleasant task because it had been her idea. The guys stayed for a while and Carrie had a wonderful time with Pete. Mandy noticed again how kind he was, but never once did he give Carrie a false impression, something for which Mandy was very grateful.

There was no opportunity for Ross and Mandy to speak privately and finish the conversation they had started on the walk home. Because Mandy was upset about the evening, the air around the two of them was a little more strained.

Mandy climbed gratefully into bed that night with one thought on her mind. Tomorrow was Monday, and Silas and Amy were coming home.

48

"I'm glad you're back."

"Well, you can look a little more excited when you say it, Luke," Silas commented dryly, and then became alert to the serious look on his brother's face.

"Thursday night I thought I heard noises over by your house, but when I stood at my bedroom window things looked quiet. It was a little windy and I blamed that. For my own peace of mind I came over Friday morning. Nothing looked out of order, but this was laying by your back steps."

Reaching to a high shelf in the barn where the men stood, Luke picked up a cigar stub and handed it to Silas.

"None of our buyers ever go near your house, Si. If I'd found this by the barn, I'd have thought nothing of it. So I went on in, but nothing looked out of order and I'm sure I would have noticed with the way Amy keeps things."

Silas was praying as Luke spoke, his heart pounding at the thought of some stranger in his home. Something was not right. The cigar was certainly no reason to go off the deep end. But Silas had the most uncomfortable feeling that someone had been looking for the papers Mandy said she was taking to Grandma Em's for Ross to see. He had no idea from where the thought came. It was just there and would not go away.

Silas' first temptation, to ride directly in and talk to the sheriff, was abating as he stood with his brother and continued to pray silently.

"What will you do?"

"For right now, I'll wait and pray." He put the stub in his coat pocket and looked at Luke. "I don't want to overreact or scare anyone, but something isn't right." Silas then explained briefly about the papers Ross had said he wanted to see and how with the trip he hadn't taken any of it too seriously. He hadn't even asked Mandy if he could look at the papers.

"Then Ross still has them?"

"Just the document about the land agreement with this guy from Reedsburg. I heard Amy ask Mandy about it. Mandy said Ross returned everything but that. Amy also questioned her about the reading of her mother's diary, and Mandy said she read some more on the weekend but was nowhere near through it."

"Amy doesn't ask questions just because she's nosy."

"No, she doesn't, and I think I'd better check with her and see what she's thinking."

The chance did not come for Silas until husband and wife had retired for the night. Silas told Amy about Luke hearing something Thursday night and then showed her the cigar stub.

"Do you really think someone was in the house?"

"I don't know. Like Luke said, nothing was disturbed."

Silas watched as Amy checked her jewelry box. He'd already done the same thing this afternoon and told her as much.

"Why didn't you tell me earlier?"

"Because you and I haven't been alone until now, and I don't want to scare the kids."

"Are you going to report it?"

"Not right now. Amy, tell me what you were thinking when you asked Mandy about reading the diary and her mother's papers."

"It's not very nice." Silas' brows raised but he waited without comment, watching her as she stood by the dresser.

"Silas, I don't like town gossip. I try never to get involved."

"Right," Silas said carefully, waiting for her to come to the point.

"I think Aaron Marks is a liar and a cheat!"

Most people would have considered this mild, but Silas knew better. Amy was one of the kindest, least judgmental persons he had ever met. It was not her habit to call people names or be vindictive; in fact, Silas was sure this was the first time he'd ever heard her do so. She looked so troubled after admitting her thoughts that he held out his arms to her from the bed. She didn't hesitate, and as always Silas' heart turned over when she was cuddled against him.

"Silas," she continued after a few moments. "I don't want anything for the kids that doesn't rightfully belong to them, but if Aaron Marks cheated Ward Jackson to get that land—and I can't help but think that he did—then I think we should do everything we can to get it back."

"Why don't we ask Christine to take Becca tomorrow morning? After the kids leave for school, you and I can take Mandy in and see Ross. We'll talk about everything we *know* to be true as well as the things we feel *might* be true. He'll tell us if we should drop the whole thing and accept that the land is gone, or go to Rufus with our concerns.

"It seems like I've taken more than my fair share of time off, but when Luke and I talked today he said that now is the time to get this cleared up. I can't help but agree with him."

Just after Silas stopped talking there was a knock on the door.

"Come in," Amy called.

"I heard you talking," Mandy said as she came in, her words tumbling out faster than Silas and Amy had ever heard. "I needed a drink of water and I saw your light. I've been reading in Mama's dairy, and I found something that clears up Pa's letter to me, or at least part of it."

"Here, let's see." Silas held out his hand and Mandy scooted over to the edge of the bed to give it to him. She stood beside the bed, the front of her flannel nightgown clutched in her fists.

Silas read—"We went on a picnic today out in the bluffs. Ward told the children their favorite story this time at butterfly rock. He lifted the girls up to touch the 'butterfly' and Carrie squealed in delight. I wish Ward could be here more. I think I might be pregnant again."

Both Silas and Amy looked in question at Mandy. "I remember now. Pa used to tell us a story about a beautiful butterfly who made a deal with the sun, a deal that the sun would shine on the butterfly every day and keep him warm enough to survive all winter. The sun agreed to the plan but warned the butterfly that he must always remember who it was that gave him winter life and give the credit where credit was due. If the butterfly broke the deal, he would be turned into stone.

"Pa always dragged it out and made it really long but this day, the day Mama writes about in the diary, was the first time he took us to a place in the bluffs and showed us a rock that actually looks like a butterfly. Pa said the butterfly sat fluttering his wings and bragged to a fox who had to hibernate in the winter. He was instantly transformed into the rock, exactly like the ones he was resting on. It all came back as I read the diary. I remember it like it was yesterday.

"My pa's letter," she opened her hand where she'd been crushing it in her excitement, "said to remember the stories around butterfly rock. He took us there about three times. The letter said the rock would help us."

Silas took the letter and read it himself. "And you know where this rock is?"

"The exact spot."

"On Aaron Marks' land." Amy said the words quietly and there was a very definite look of defeat on Mandy's face. Silas explained to her what their plan was for the morning, and Mandy agreed wholeheartedly.

Silas kept the diary and letter with him in the bedroom that night. In the morning, the three of them headed for Ross Beckett's office.

49

It was a terrible letdown to find Ross' office empty. They swung by his house but it too was quiet. Silas stopped at the bank and asked Pete to tell Ross that he, Amy, and Mandy would be at Grandma Em's for a while and hoped to see him.

Mandy had turned into a bundle of nerves when Ross arrived 45 minutes later.

"Mandy, why don't you sit down?" Grandma Em suggested softly and Mandy did sit for just a few moments as Silas explained why they had come into town. But she was up again in no time at all, pacing around the end of the living room.

Ross' face was grave as he read the diary and then the letter. When Silas produced the cigar stub, he came forward on his chair and reached for it.

"This is the same type as those Amanda's father smoked." He said the words thoughtfully and almost to himself, but Mandy had heard.

"My pa didn't smoke."

Ross stared at her and then back at the cigar. "Not ever?"

"No, at least not at home, and I can't think why he would have kept it hidden from us."

"Amanda," Ross' voice was quiet, intense. "The day you drove the wagon home and then went in and found the picture of your mother, there was a cigar stub just like this on the floor of the bedroom. I didn't give any thought to it because I assumed it was your father's."

Mandy's eyes had grown very wide. "I noticed a funny smell when I went in that day. I thought it was because we hadn't been there and the air was stale. Also a letter that I know Mama got from Pa last winter was not with her things."

"Another cigar stub was laying outside the day we went to move the furniture," Ross added to this new information. "But Aaron Marks had already arrived and I can't remember if the cigar had been there before he was or not. And then, of course, I was still thinking they were your father's, so I didn't give much thought to it."

"Do we have enough information to take to Rufus?"

"Yes, Silas, we do. But whether he'll agree to a search warrant or an investigation of any kind remains to be seen."

Everything was laid out on the kitchen table after that, and Ross and Silas went over every inch of what they had. The document from Mr. Brooks, the letter, the diary, all of it was read and reread. They exhausted every avenue, Ross taking notes all the while. Then he gathered the papers and put them in a flat, black case. Mandy, who had paced through most of their examination, touched his arm.

"My things, they'll be safe? I mean, I have so little that was my parents'."

"I'll return everything to you, Amanda. Now try to stop fretting."

"Ross," Amy spoke for the first time. "I probably don't need to say this, but we don't want to do anything illegal."

"I understand what you mean, and we may run up against that very wall in our effort to investigate this within the bounds of the law. If Marks does actually own the Jackson land, and this butterfly rock is on that land, then our hands are basically tied.

"I'm headed right now to see Rufus. Why don't I come out to the house tonight and tell you what I come up with today?"

After this plan was agreed upon, Grandma Em walked Silas and Amy to the wagon. Mandy was about to follow when Ross called her name and took her arm.

"I'll do what I can for you, Amanda."

"I know you will, Ross, and I appreciate it."

"You didn't say much today. What do you think is significant about butterfly rock?"

"There are a lot of little holes and even some caves in that area. I think Pa hid something and hoped that I would understand where to look."

Ross nodded, having come to the same conclusion. He stared down at the woman before him and felt cheated that he'd seen so little of her lately. He'd prayed much about his relationship with her and had come to some very startling, humbling decisions which he wanted desperately to share with her when the time was right.

"Maybe when this is cleared up a bit, we can talk."

"I'd like that." As always when she looked at him, her heart beat faster. He permeated her thoughts, and although she begged God to change her feelings, she was still head-over-heels in love with Ross Beckett.

Out at the wagon Silas looked as if he might walk back in search of Mandy.

"Give them a few minutes, Si."

The tall man looked at his grandmother.

"I remember sitting across the table from a certain grandson a few years ago, when he'd just come back from Neillsville *without* the woman he loved." Grandma Em smiled at Amy before she continued.

"Ross and Mandy have the same miserable expressions you wore when you didn't know if the person you loved would ever be yours. We're told that in Christ we can be made whole and that in Him we need nothing else. But when we find the one we think we can't live without, it's pretty hard finding joy with that person out of reach. I'm not saying you can't do it; it just doesn't come easily."

"And you think Ross and Mandy should be together?" Amy wanted to know.

"You might think I'm a meddling old woman, and I speak only for myself, not what the Lord wants—but yes, I think they should be together."

— ⁜ —

"This is one of the things I appreciate about you, Ross," Rufus spoke with sincerity, "you work with the law. I know what I've said frustrates you, but you will not set foot on that land! Everything you've showed me looks bad, and you're right, the worst thing we could do right now is to alert Marks to our suspicions. All the more reason for you to let me handle it.

"Go ahead and get in touch with this Brooks in Reedsburg and see what he has to say. I'll do a bit of scouting around. Marks wouldn't dare throw me off his place."

"I hear he's actually living out there."

"Yeah, one of the nicest homes in Baxter and Marks chooses to live in a shack at the edge of town. It makes you wonder.

"Now, you've got to warn Silas and the family that this is not going to fall into place overnight. Let me know when Brooks gets back to you. Meanwhile I'll be keeping my eyes open for anything suspicious."

Ross had hoped for a more encouraging report to take to Mandy that night, but it was not to be. She was grateful nonetheless, and Ross prayed for patience over having things constantly crop up to keep him and Amanda apart.

50

Things seemed to come to a standstill after the day Ross met with Rufus. Nothing suspicious turned up and no reply came from Reedsburg. Ross even inquired a second time and continued to wait.

October came and by the middle of the month temperatures plummeted. No one was mentally prepared for the snow flurries that came one afternoon. Grandma Em wished the only storm in her world was outside.

"Well, Preston, what brings you out on such a cold day?"

Emily Cameron opened the door wide for just an instant to allow him in. She took his coat and asked him if he cared for coffee.

"Is everything alright, Emily?" he asked when she set his cup in front of him.

"I'm a little tired today. I'm sorry about the black coffee, I'm out of sugar." She said the words hoping she sounded casual, but Preston's eyes were watchful and Grandma Em wondered if maybe the Lord had sent him just so she could talk with someone.

The truth was Preston knew exactly why she was upset, but Emily was a woman of dignity and and he didn't want to do anything to destroy that quality. Telling her of his nephew's visit this morning to inform him of yesterday's talk with Grandma Em might ruin the trust she had in the bank.

"Preston, have you ever worried that when you grew very old you would be a burden to your family?"

"It's crossed my mind some." He watched her stare distractedly out the window while she fiddled with the handle on her still-full coffee cup.

"Pride is a terrible thing, isn't it? I've made a mistake, and the thought of my grandchildren finding out and thinking I'm failing, well, let's just say that wounds my pride."

"Do you want to tell me about the mistake?"

She looked at him for a long time before sliding a ledger across the table to him. Preston turned the pages slowly and was glad Pete had warned him. Emily Cameron's savings were near depletion.

"I can't think how I did it. To go along for years thinking I've got sufficient savings to live out my life, and then to find out it's nowhere near enough...Peter showed me several errors, do you see them? They wouldn't have been so bad by themselves but Joseph's original entry, in error by several hundred dollars, is the one that really hurts.

"Preston, I know that the Lord will take care of me and I know that the children would step in without question, but I just hate the thought of telling them. My pride, I guess, or not wanting to be a burden, I don't know which."

"My timing is probably terrible but maybe now is the time to ask that question I've been hoping you'll say yes to." Preston's voice was soft and deep, his eyes intent on her face.

"And have you think I'm saying yes because I'm running out of money?" Obviously the idea appalled her.

"I know better, Emily. And I also believe God will take care of you. But did you ever stop to think *I* might be God's answer to your needs?"

She hated the tears that flooded her eyes on that question, but they would not be stopped. Preston's arms were around her as they stood by the table and Emily Cameron couldn't remember anything ever feeling so wonderful. She'd forgotten how marvelous it was to be held and feel protected within the arms of a man who loves you.

"Everything is going to be fine, Emily. I'll see to that." The words were said as Preston held her tight, and all her doubts evaporated.

— ✥ —

"I can't believe that the pond is actually frozen."

"That's what everyone is saying, Ross."

Ross shook his head in amazement. The weather was cold, very cold, and had been for what seemed like weeks, but it being only the first of November, it just didn't feel like winter.

"There's talk of an ice-skating party. Pastor Chad and one of the elders are planning to see if it's safe on the ice, not that the big pond is very deep."

"When would this be?"

"Saturday afternoon."

Ross nodded in contemplation. He and Pete were headed out to Silas' tonight and an idea was forming in his head; he would ask Amanda to the skating party. If it turned out they didn't go, he would ask her to supper at the hotel.

"You know, for a lawyer, you don't work very hard at keeping your thoughts off your face. You're grinning like a fool."

"I'm not trying to hide my thoughts."

"Let me guess, you're thinking of Mandy?"

"How did you know?" Ross was truly surprised. "I don't even see her, except for Sundays."

"Ah, but Ross, it's the evidence I see on Sundays that gives you away," Pete said with a cheeky grin.

"What evidence?" Ross demanded.

But Pete only laughed and reminded Ross they were going to be late for supper if they didn't get ready to go.

Ross was glad for the respite but didn't begin cleaning up the minute his door was closed. He needed a few minutes alone to think about all that had happened.

He had not had one moment alone with Mandy since the short conversation in Grandma Em's living room over a month ago. In all of the Sunday dinners and birthdays, he hadn't the slightest chance to speak privately with her. And why he never asked for such an opportunity, like suggesting dinner or a drive, was beyond him at the moment.

Well, starting tonight all that would change. He really hoped that this land matter with Aaron Marks would be settled, so that Mandy would not feel that a part of her life was hanging in the balance. But at the moment that was not happening and Ross, who believed he had clear leading from the Lord, was not going to wait any longer.

51

"What has come over Peter?" Mandy whispered to Ross in confusion as soon as they were in the kitchen alone.

Ross shrugged his shoulders, thinking as he did that he was going to murder his housemate and leave his body to freeze in the snow.

If Pete had made one reference tonight about Ross and Mandy being a nice couple, he'd made 50. Comments such as "Ross, I think Mandy needs the potatoes," when they were sitting at *Silas'* elbow were nonstop. Neither Silas or Amy seemed upset by his words or actions, but Ross, who had tossed him more than one quelling look, wanted to get his hands around Pete's neck.

Now supper was over and Ross was helping clear the table. He watched Mandy sail back out to the dining room for more dishes and followed on her heels.

Minutes later Mandy came very close to dropping her load of plates on the kitchen floor when Pete's voice came through from the dining room.

"Here, Amy, I'll get those. Mandy and Ross can do dishes and I'll help clear."

"I can help them, Pete," Carrie's voice spoke after a moment. Mandy didn't hear the reply, but Carrie joined them in the kitchen a few minutes later.

"You know this kitchen isn't as large as I thought." Carrie and Mandy stared at Pete, who was coming into the kitchen with the last stack of plates, as though he'd sprouted wings. "I really think, Carrie, that Ross and Mandy would have more room to work if you were out of here."

Mandy's mouth dropped open when Pete winked at her and whisked Carrie out of the kitchen before anyone could object. Her eyes filled with suspicion, Mandy looked to Ross.

"Do you want to wash or dry?" His voice was as calm as you please, but his gaze was watchful.

Hesitating before she answered, Mandy hoped that something on his face would tell her what was going on.

"Carrie can come back in and help."

"I don't mind," Ross assured her.

"I'll wash then," Mandy said after a moment and began to shave the bar of soap into the pan.

"Had you heard about the skating party Saturday?"

"At the pond you mean?" Mandy deliberately kept her voice neutral.

"Yeah."

"I think Silas and Amy plan for us to go."

"Actually, I was hoping you would accompany me."

Mandy's hands stilled in the soapy water and she turned slowly to face Ross. His hands were motionless on the plate he'd been drying, his eyes intent, hers questioning.

"You scare me to death, Amanda," he spoke softly. "Not you specifically, but the thought of disappointing you. I've never met anyone who was in such need of cherishing. From the moment I met you I wanted to be the one to have that job, but all I've done is hurt you."

"That's not true, Ross."

"Maybe not completely, but I have hurt you and the reason wasn't clear until recently. I was trying to meet your needs in and of myself, trying to be too much to you. I didn't want to get involved until I was sure of never hurting you or disappointing you again. But that was my idea, not God's.

"There will be hurts and disappointments because I'm human, but Amanda, it won't mean that I don't care. In Christ I know you'll forgive me.

"I thought that when the land was settled we could begin seeing each other, but it's taking longer than expected and I want to get to know you *now*. I want to see and be with you *now*. If that sounds selfish, I'm sorry. Maybe all of this is too sudden." Ross watched her a moment, wondering if he was about to be rejected.

"Is it too sudden, Amanda?"

Ross watched her hair swing against her shoulders as she shook her head no.

He would have understood if she didn't trust him, but he really believed they had a future together and it had to start somewhere. The simple movement of her head made his heart fill and made speech a little difficult.

"Amanda, will you go skating with me Saturday afternoon?"

"I'd like that, Ross, very much.

52

Ross combed his hair for what must have been the fifth time and then laughed when he remembered he'd be wearing a hat the entire time they skated. The thermometer had risen some, but it was by no means warm. At least the sun was shining and it would be light for a few more hours.

Preston and Grandma Em would be coming any minute, and he had already heard Pete go downstairs. In less than ten minutes he would see Amanda. The thought made his heart pound. He wanted very much to give her time, but he also knew he was going to kiss her if the moment presented itself this evening.

He had done a tremendous amount of pondering on kissing in the last few days and had come to some serious conclusions, the most important being, you don't kiss a woman unless you're going to marry her.

He had kissed Sarah the times he'd gone away, and done so in the strongest belief that she would someday be his wife. For that reason he felt no shame. But the two other girls, the ones he had kissed before he came to Christ, brought him grief. Both girls had married men from his hometown, and Ross was profoundly sorry he'd kissed another man's wife. That they were unmarried when he kissed them was beside the point. Faithfulness began even before you met your intended.

Ross suddenly wondered if Mandy had ever kissed a man. He knew for the first time, in that instant, that he was capable of jealousy. He didn't feel enraged, but the thought of someone else kissing his Amanda was not a pleasant one. When the time was right he would apologize to her about the girls before he was saved and explain about Sarah. And if she had kissed other men he would need to feel the same forgiveness *for* her as he wanted *from* her.

"Ross, are you coming?" Pete called from the stairway. Ross hit the door at a run, his hat and gloves in hand.

— ✦ —

"We couldn't have asked for a clearer day," Amy said as their wagon pulled up to the pond. There were two bonfires blazing to ward off the cold and to heat the cocoa, the aroma of which was already filling the air.

"Let's get cocoa." Levi's first love was his stomach.

"You're supposed to wait until you're a little colder. We just got here," Carrie informed her brother even as the four youngest Jacksons started that way.

"Mandy, honey, I'm a little worried about you," Silas spoke with a gleam in his eyes. "You look so depressed this afternoon."

Mandy laughed at his teasing which made her sparkling eyes even brighter, if that were possible. Her scarf and hat were white against her navy coat, all of which framed her beautiful face and dark hair. Silas looked at her with pride, thinking a man couldn't ask for a lovelier daughter.

"You're not upset about meeting Ross here?"

"No, Silas, not at all. It didn't make any sense for him to drive all the way to our house." She spotted Ross just after she said this, and Silas watched as she bit her lower lip, much the way his wife did when she was upset. With Mandy it was uncertainty.

"Have I told you that you look wonderful?"

"Do I really, Silas?" She looked so anxious, his heart turned over.

"Yes, honey, you do. Now go and have some fun."

He watched her walk toward Preston's wagon and for an instant, felt like he was losing her. It almost gave him a feeling of being cheated. She'd lived with them such a short time.

"She's not married yet, Si," Amy read his thoughts. He smiled as he took her hand to follow the kids.

— ✦ —

"I haven't done very much of this."

"You're doing fine." Ross spoke the soothing words as he held Mandy's hand and led her out to the middle of the pond. He turned suddenly and skated backwards, taking both of her hands in his and guiding her progress.

"I thought you said you hadn't skated for years!" Accusing him, she watched him glide backward, seemingly without effort. The words were a mistake because they caused her to take her eyes off of their feet. In the next instant both skates went in different directions. Ross caught her as she started down, laughing at the surprised look on her face.

"That was close," Mandy said breathlessly.

"You didn't really think I would catch you, did you?"

"No, I guess I didn't."

"O ye of little faith." And then, "Amanda, look at me."

"I can't do that."

"Yes, you can."

"No, I'll fall.

"Then I'll catch you." But still she kept her eyes glued to the ice. Nothing he could say would make her raise them.

"You're going to get a stiff neck," Ross finally told her, but she had no chance to reply because Becca and Eliza skated into them just then and all four went down in a laughing heap.

"Becca, I thought you were going to stay with Silas."

"I was, but Eliza's helping me."

"I can see that." The skeptical tone was lost on the little girls who were once again on their skates and making unsteady progress across the pond with shrieks and giggles.

"Ross, wouldn't you rather move a little faster? I mean, just because you asked me to come with you doesn't mean you have to hold my hand the entire afternoon."

"Maybe I want to hold your hand the entire afternoon." He had her on her feet now and they stood still for a moment on the ice. Mandy loved the way he looked in his hat, especially when he pushed it back a bit on his forehead, like it was now.

Ross thought Amanda, with her white hat slightly askew, was the most adorable thing he'd ever seen. He slipped one glove off to brush a few flakes of snow on her cheek. She never took her eyes from his, as he replaced his glove and took her mittened hand, not even when Ross guided her forward across the ice.

53

The hot liquid in the cup burned Mandy's tongue a little, and she blew across the top in an effort to cool it.

"Do you want a little snow in that?"

"No thanks, I like it pretty hot."

She and Ross stood near one of the fires and watched April Nolan on the ice. April was a charming picture of controlled movement, her hands held gracefully at her sides, giving her balance as she glided along the ice.

"She's wonderful, isn't she?"

"She sure is," Ross agreed.

Mandy's attention was caught by Levi and Clovis arguing. She moved toward them just as the first snowball flew. One whizzed just past her head as she neared, and she reached for Levi before he could let another one fly.

"Levi, don't—" Mandy's words were stopped when a snowball hit her right in the chest. She looked down slowly at the white splat on her blue coat and then over at Clovis, whose eyes were wide.

The little boy was still standing transfixed by what he had done to his sister when Mandy balled up a handful of snow and threw it hard. What followed was a massive snow fight, adults, teens, and little ones all joining in to bombard one another. Some even left the ice to participate.

Ross searched for Mandy in the sea of white and laughed when he spotted her cowering behind Mac's huge form. She didn't argue when she felt a hand tug on her arm, and allowed Ross to lead her away into the shelter of two nearby trees. She leaned against one, still laughing from the fun and gasping for breath.

"How long do you think it'll go on?"

"I don't know," Ross said as he peeked out. "It's getting dark, which is going to make everyone's aim worse than it already is."

Mandy stepped away from the tree, watching with Ross from a safe distance. When she felt his eyes on her she turned her head to look at him. Dusk was quickly turning to darkness, but Ross was very aware of their lack of privacy.

"Well, you two are smart," Carrie said as she approached. "It's getting wild in there."

"Amanda figured that out a long time ago—she was hiding behind Mac earlier."

Carrie laughed out loud before her attention was captured by Pete skating with one of the girls from church. Mandy, still intent on the last snowball throwers, missed her gaze, but Ross watched her face in the waning light.

"Oh, Becca's crying and I don't see Amy. I'd better go back over." Mandy didn't wait to see if anyone followed, leaving Carrie and Ross alone.

"Does Pete have someone special in Reedsburg?"

"I don't think so."

"That wasn't really fair of me to ask you. I'm sorry."

"No need to apologize. I think I understand."

"I don't think anyone understands," Carrie told him honestly.

"You might be surprised, Carrie." His words caused her to look at him in a new light, and she saw how kind his gaze was.

"I think you might be real good for Mandy," she said after a moment, as if just realizing this.

"I'm glad you think so; your opinion means a lot to me."

"Does it really?"

"Yep," he stated firmly. Carrie was surprised speechless when he bent and kissed her forehead before following Mandy's tracks back to the pond.

— ❖ —

"Thank you, Preston. Would you like to come in? I can make us a snack." Grandma Em spoke as she took her coat from Preston's hands. Hanging it in the closet, she noticed he hadn't answered or removed his own coat.

"Preston?" she questioned softly again.

"I want to, Emily, but I think I'll pass tonight."

It was tempting to ask if she'd done something wrong, even though the entire evening had been wonderful.

"Your hands are cold." He had reached for her hands and held them gently as they stood by the front door. "Would you like me to add logs to the stove before I go?"

"I can do it."

He released her as though she hadn't spoken and went into the kitchen. Grandma Em waited where she was. Preston still had his coat on when he returned, and he went directly to the door and put his hand on the knob.

A minute passed before he changed his mind and moved away from the door. With his hand beneath Emily's chin, he raised her face and gently brushed her lips with his own. Raising his head he studied her face as if memorizing every feature in the lamplight.

In the next moment he said good-bye and moved out the door, his mind contemplating and praying about what he'd seen in Emily's eyes.

54

The next morning Ross moved up the aisle of the church with Pete and did not immediately see Silas and Amy in their pew. After he sat down, he spotted the person he had been searching for and considered moving up to sit next to Amanda. Just as he made up his mind to move, Candy Hunter slid into the pew and blocked his path. His smile to her was strained, but she didn't seem to notice.

He moved toward Pete as subtly as he could, but then two more girls joined them on the end of the row. Once again he was nearly shoulder to shoulder with Candy.

Ross began to fiddle with the binding on his Bible and didn't notice when Mandy turned in her pew, noticing him sitting with another girl.

Mandy told herself she was not going to jump to conclusions. The way they were all seated it *did* look like the girls sat with the boys and not the other way around. Maybe Ross just hadn't seen her.

The sermon was lost on Mandy that morning, no matter how hard she tried to concentrate. Visions of the evening before floated through her mind—Ross holding her hand, Ross brushing snow from her face, Ross looking at her with loving eyes, and then Ross telling her at the end of the evening that he would be at Grandma Em's tomorrow for dinner. He made the words sound like a promise.

He had walked her to Silas' wagon when everyone was leaving the pond, and Mandy wished she could have asked him to come back to the house with them for a while. But she was afraid of looking pushy so she sat in the wagon and watched him go over to Preston's sleigh. She comforted herself with the knowledge that tomorrow was Sunday, so she would see him at church as well as at Grandma Em's.

Their wagon was well on its way before Mandy saw they were headed in the wrong direction. Disappointment knifed

230

through her when she remembered they'd been asked to Sunday dinner at Pastor Chad and Aunt April's. But Mandy was not one to sulk, so she joined in with the preparation and cleanup. If once in a while her thoughts seemed a little far away, no one appeared to notice. But April and Amy shared more than one glance when they noticed Mandy's attention waning. Mandy seemed relieved when a few games were brought out and she was able to shift her attention to the here and now.

Ross was in the same miserable condition a few blocks away. He first waited for Silas and Amy's wagon to arrive and then tried to eat a plate full of food for which he was not in the least bit hungry.

Was it normal to be so miserable when you found yourself in love? The question kept coming to mind. And how about the lack of privacy? Ross wanted to kiss Mandy and hold her in his arms and tell her he loved her.

His mind dwelt on the way she always looked up at him with those big hazel eyes, waiting for him to make the first move. Eyes that were still just a little bit wary, a little bit fearful of being rejected.

"Oh, I forgot to give April this music," Grandma Em was saying as the table was being cleared in the kitchen. "She needs it for next Sunday."

Ross was all ears, and though he could feel his heart quicken, his stance beside the door never altered.

"Is there something I can do?" he asked quietly.

"Yes there is, if you would. There's no hurry but if you could drop these at Chad and April's on your way home, I'd really appreciate it. On the other hand, if you left now, you wouldn't miss Mandy." She spoke these final words to Ross alone, and he could see she had just thought of it.

Ross kissed her cheek and took the music. His smile was almost one of relief. When he'd gone out the door, Calvin, the only other one in the room spoke.

"He's in love."

"Now, what makes you so sure of that, Cal?" His great-grandmother wanted to know.

"He acts just like Luke did a few years ago with Christine. You know, not really listening when you talk to him and playing with his food instead of eating it. Come to think of it, Gram, you didn't eat much today either. You feel okay?"

"I feel fine, Cal," she told him with a smile. "Just fine."

— ❖ —

"Am I ever glad to see you," Carrie said to Ross as she answered the kitchen door. "Mandy's been in a cloud all day."

"Who is it, Carrie? Oh, hi Ross," Pastor Chad greeted him.

"Hello, Pastor. Grandma Em asked me to bring Mrs. Nolan this music."

"Oh fine, come on in and give it to her."

"No, wait," Carrie whispered. "Ross, you stay here. I'll send Mandy out here for something and you can surprise her."

Pastor Nolan chuckled as Carrie dragged Ross over to the wall next to the door. Ross was looking a little baffled by the whole charade when Carrie and Pastor Nolan went out and shut the door.

It took several minutes before the door opened. Ross had begun to think he had been forgotten. Mandy came in and plucked a coffee mug from one of the hooks on the wall, nearly dropping it when she turned to find him standing there. She put the mug on the table and stood still, content just to look at him.

Ross hadn't even been given time to take off his hat and coat. Mandy watched as he pushed his hat back on his head, his eyes seeming to memorize everything about her. She watched as he stripped the glove off one hand and beckoned to her with the crook of one finger.

Mandy didn't need to be asked twice. She walked slowly toward him and stopped when she was close. "I forgot we were invited here today," she said softly.

"I figured as much," he answered, equally soft. "I didn't spot you in church until after I'd sat down, and then the pew filled up and I couldn't come up and sit with you."

"I figured as much."

No other words were necessary as Ross slipped his other glove off and tossed it toward the table without taking his eyes from Mandy. His hands came up to frame her face, his thumbs gently tracing Mandy's cheekbones. Her eyes slid shut at his touch and then flew open when his lips brushed hers.

"Am I out of line?" he questioned her softly, his eyes holding hers, his lips just a breath away.

"No," she breathed as she raised her face invitingly, her eyes closing once again.

Ross needed no further prompting. Both of them were surprised a moment later to see that Silas had come into the room. No apology was made and Ross slipped his arm around Mandy as they turned to face Silas.

Silas stood for a moment and looked at them. He knew in that instant what other people saw when they looked at him and Amy—a couple in love.

"Hello, Ross." Silas put his hand out and Ross shook it. "I hope you'll stay for coffee."

"I will, thanks."

Mandy saw the gesture for what it was: approval. She left Ross' side and went on tiptoe to kiss Silas' cheek. He hugged her close and then teased her about the coffee she was supposed to be bringing him.

Within minutes the kitchen was filled with Camerons, Nolans, Jacksons, and one Beckett. They were all waiting for coffee or hot chocolate. They were snitching the spice cake that was supposed to be enjoyed with the coffee, as well as the sliced apples that had been put on the table.

Becca plopped down in Ross' lap and gave him bites of her apple. He kissed her cheek on one of those occasions and her little hand flew to that spot as she looked at him with adoring eyes.

Mandy was pleased to see that the man she loved was accepted and loved by her family. When Levi got a bigger piece of cake, Ross traded with Clovis to avoid an argument. It was a little thing really, but everyone noticed and appreciated his thoughtfulness. His eyes, when anyone spoke to him, were attentive and respectful, but no one could help notice the change in them when they turned to focus on Mandy.

They said she was the most wonderful, beautiful, desirable woman on earth and that he loved her. They said how important she was to him and that he cared for her happiness and welfare.

And Mandy's eyes said no less to Ross. She looked at him as if he were the answer to her prayers. And as a life mate, he was.

The afternoon was wonderful, and Mandy and Ross parted with the promise that Ross would come for supper the next night. Mandy came close to forgetting to thank Aunt April and Uncle Chad for their hospitality, so mindful was she of Ross' riding away.

Again everyone was tolerant and almost amused. It was quite obvious to all of them that Ross and Mandy had a future together.

55

Almost two weeks had passed, and every afternoon when Ross closed his office, he could be seen headed in the direction of the Cameron ranch. Ross and Mandy grew closer each time they were together, and Ross made mental plans to take Mandy home to meet his parents after Christmas. He admitted as much to Pete.

"Christmas? I thought you were in love with this girl."

"I am."

"Then what are you waiting for? I honestly thought we'd be having a Thanksgiving wedding around here, January at the latest."

Ross looked thoughtful and then very pleased with himself. He slapped Pete on the shoulder. "Thanks, Pete. I need to go see Grandma Em. I'll see you later." Ross had only been gone for a few minutes when Pete answered a knock at the door.

"Hello, I'm looking for Ross Beckett."

"Come in. He's not here right now, but maybe there's something I can do for you?"

"Who are you?"

"Peter Culver." Pete's hand went out and the men shook. "Ross and I live here together. And you are—"

"The name's Brooks. I've come over from Reedsburg about my land."

— ✣ —

"Here it is, Ross." Grandma Em held out a beautiful gold chain with a gold heart hanging from it, set with a small white pearl. Ross reached for it and smiled.

"Thanks for keeping it for me. I'm sure I would have lost it in the move."

"You say it was your grandmother's?"

"Yes. She's no longer living but my mother will recognize it the first time she sees Amanda. You do think Amanda will like it, don't you?" He looked so unsure that Grandma Em laughed.

"She'll love it. Are you going to ask her tonight?"

"Yep. I hope she'll have me."

"Somehow I doubt you'll have any trouble convincing her of your love."

They smiled at each other, and Ross started for the front door when Pete stuck his head in.

"Sorry to intrude, Grandma Em, but I had to catch Ross." Pete turned to him. "There's a man here who I'm sure you'll want to meet."

"Come in, Peter, please," Grandma Em said graciously.

She and Ross stood back as Pete entered with a man in his forties. Pete introduced the man as Larry Brooks of Reedsburg.

"I'm here about my land," he said without preamble. "I need to see you and Aaron Marks to see if I can make this clear—*my land is not for sale!*"

— ❖ —

"Clovis, Levi, I've asked you not to run through the house." Amy's voice checked their stride in the kitchen, but they ran again as soon as they were out of sight, calling back as they went, "Ross is here."

"Ross?" Mandy and Amy looked at one another because it was a good two hours to supper. The boys had left the front door wide open and were on the porch without coats when the women arrived on the scene.

"Boys, come in here," Mandy called to them. They obeyed reluctantly and only because Ross was almost on the porch and bringing with him a visitor.

The men were welcomed inside, but before Ross could make any introductions, Mandy spoke.

"Hello, Mr. Brooks. It's nice to see you."

"Well, hello, young lady. You're looking well." He smiled, his eyes twinkling, as if they shared some private joke.

Introductions were then made. When she heard that Ross and Mr. Brooks were here on business, Amy sent the boys out to the barn for Silas.

By the time Silas arrived and met Mr. Brooks, the men had a map laid out on the dining room table along with legal papers, some familiar.

"I discovered the mistake just a few months ago when there was such sudden interest in my land. Marks contacted me, as did a lawyer in Reedsburg and you, too." Larry Brooks pointed a finger at Ross.

"I would have come over here sooner, certainly before we had snow on the ground, but I've been sick and couldn't get away. Not that it would have made any difference about this contract with Marks." Mr. Brooks turned to Mandy and her siblings who were gathered close by.

"Your father was no family man, but I guess you already know that. But he loved you—I know he did. We talked on several occasions and my willingness to buy the land was, in his opinion, money in the bank. That money he always said, belonged to you kids and your mother.

"I guess that's why I find it hard to believe Ward would sign the contract with Marks that Ross described to me. Not that I can do anything about it," he said regretfully.

"The main reason I'm here is because I don't like the way Marks does business. You see, he wrote to me. Asked about my land, said something about studying rocks or some such nonsense. Well, I thought it pretty harmless until a lawyer showed up at my door and said he was working for Aaron Marks and did I want to sell my property in Baxter. I could see the man was not satisfied with the answers I gave him about selling, and I found evidence the next day that someone had tried to break into my safe.

"I got sick a few days after that, or like I said, I'd have been over here much sooner."

"But what's the mistake you mentioned?" Mandy wanted to know.

"It's here on the map, the original map. The boundaries on our properties are wrong. I actually own this section of land with the rock here." He pointed to the map.

"Believe me, Mandy, I'd have never said a word if your folks were still alive, but I don't trust Aaron Marks and I want to make sure he's not building anything on my land."

"Did you give him permission to be on your land at all?" Ross asked.

"No, I did not! His lawyer showed up before I could answer, and after the incident with the safe I wrote and told him *no*, my land is not for sale and to keep off it. I said it just that plainly, too!"

Ross looked over at the woman he loved to find her leaning over the map studying it intently. As though everyone in the room sensed her concentration, all were quiet. Some minutes went by before her attention swung to the dark windows and then to Mr. Brooks.

"Mr. Brooks, did Ross tell you about the letter my father sent to me just before he died?"

"He mentioned it, yes. Said you wished you could go to a rock he referred to and look around."

"That's right. We thought it was Aaron Marks' land, but I don't think it is."

"Mandy, what have you discovered?" Carrie asked and touched her sister's arm.

"I think butterfly rock is on the land Mr. Brooks says is lawfully his. And I want to go there in the morning."

Ross let himself quietly into the house and made his way up the stairs. Pete, who had been in the kitchen, came out to call up to him.

"How did it go?"

"We're headed out to the property in the morning."

"And the question I suspect you were going to ask Mandy?"

Ross didn't answer. Pete watched him lean against the stair wall, his look pensive.

"I know this needs to be worked out, Pete, and I'm really pleased that Brooks has come, but I was headed out there to declare myself and it's just—"

"A letdown," Pete finished for him, his voice compassionate. Ross nodded and Pete went on.

"I won't say I know how you feel, Ross, but she'll be there tomorrow or the next day or whenever the time is right. That girl is crazy about you, and I'm sure you'll agree that she's worth any amount of time you have to wait."

Ross nodded, thanked his best friend and took himself off to bed.

56

It was a large group that headed for Larry Brooks' land the next morning. Mr. Brooks, Silas, Ross, Mandy, Carrie, and Rufus, Baxter's sheriff. All gathered at the designated spot a little before eight o'clock.

The sky was clear and the snow not too deep. But the air was frigid so everyone was bundled to their eyes in an effort to keep out the cold.

By unspoken consent Mandy led the way. Her memory was keen and with very little searching she took the group down a snowy path that led between the rocks.

"Mandy," came Carrie's muffled voice as she clutched at her sister's coat, excitement surging through her as she recognized her surroundings.

The group came to a silent halt in a small clearing, and solemnly watched as the girls gazed at the rock they hadn't seen for years.

A near-perfect butterfly with outstretched wings greeted their eyes. The ledges kept the snow blocked and all but one corner of the wings showed perfectly.

Both girls felt tears sting their eyes, and their mittened hands met. The years slipped by in their minds and they were once again little girls on a summer picnic with Mama and Pa at their family's secret spot.

Mandy's memory was serving her well and she moved, almost instinctively, around the side of the rock to a good-sized opening. She had just ducked her head to enter when a hand stopped her.

"Mandy, I wanted to remind you of what I said as I left last night. This is my land, but whatever you find in that cave is yours. Just as your father would have wanted."

"Thank you, Mr. Brooks."

"Amanda." Ross' voice stopped her when she turned again to enter the cave. "I'll go first."

Mandy didn't object. Ross, Silas, and Mandy entered the cave and stood quietly out of the wind waiting for Silas to light the lantern. He turned it high and stared at the illuminated cavern, about 15 feet wide and as yet, impenetrably dark at the back. Silas started forward.

Five minutes later the three of them exited the cave, Silas carrying a small chest.

"Look what we've found!" Silas exlcaimed. "The cave looked empty at first, but Ross spotted some loose rock on the floor. Right above it was a small ledge cut into the cave wall."

Mr. Brooks was holding a shovel that Silas had brought along. He handed it to Rufus, who used the handle to pound the lock. The wind had picked up and even though the clearing was sheltered, it whistled and whipped above them in an eerie whine.

Again, by an unspoken vote, Mandy took the lead. She removed the lock, flipped the catch, and opened the lid. The group stood speechless. The small chest was laden with pouches. The top of one pouch was open and the group stared in silent fascination at the sparkling nuggets and dust. Gold!

Mandy's hand moved out to pull at some papers at the edge of the chest. She and Carrie looked at them before passing them to Ross and Silas.

"They're claim deeds. One in your father's name and one in Aaron Marks' name."

"And look here," Ross added. "Marks' is stamped worthless."

"I'll take that." The group turned as one at the sound of Aaron Marks' voice. He held a rifle and Rufus' own gun was out before anyone could blink. Ross and Silas simultaneously reached for the girls and pushed each behind them.

"We don't want any trouble, Marks," Ross told him, never once taking his eyes from the gun or the man holding it.

"Then what are you doing on my land?"

"It's not your land," Larry Brooks spoke up. "And I can prove it."

"You'll get your chance, but not out here and not with guns." Rufus' tone was firm, almost angry.

Everyone watched Marks for his decision on the sheriff's words. They were all surprised when he nodded and led the way back to the wagon and horses.

— ⁂ —

"You mean it's really ours?" Levi asked in shock.

"Yes, it's ours. Silas put it all in the bank," Carrie answered as she stood by the bed, where a pale Mandy, who was drained of all energy and thought, lay.

"I was so worried when you were gone all that time," Amy added as she put her arm around Silas. "I was afraid something like this might happen."

"I'm just sorry it had to end the way it did. It really looked as if Marks was going to be reasonable, but when he realized the gold wasn't his, he went for his gun. It was hidden up his sleeve."

Amy bent over Mandy's bed with a quilt in her hand. "Maybe if I took your shoes off you could sleep."

"I don't want to sleep. Every time I close my eyes I can see that gun pointed at me."

The scene played again in Carrie's mind—the papers on Ross' desk, the men discussing everything so calmly, and then Mr. Marks getting furious. Before anyone could move, a gun appeared in his hand. He shouted something at Mandy about it being her fault. The bullet would have caught her in the chest if Ross had not thrown himself at her and moved them both out of the way. The sheriff's gun was out in the next instant and Mr. Marks crumpled to the floor.

Silas had left everything in Ross' hands then, bringing his girls directly home.

Mandy's room emptied a little while later, but sleep did not come. "It's over now," her heart spoke to the Lord. "Thank You for taking care of us."

Mandy eventually drifted off to sleep with verses about God's protective care moving gently through her mind.

57

"Welcome back." Ross' deep voice was quiet as he watched Mandy open her eyes. She turned her head on the pillow to see him sitting beside her bed.

Unbidden, tears filled her eyes, and her hands came up to cover her face. Ross was instantly beside her, sitting carefully on the edge of the bed and taking her in his arms.

"Oh Ross, Ross," was all she could say, and he felt her tremble. His own heart was none too steady when he again envisioned the gun pointed at her.

"I keep seeing it," she finally said.

"I do, too."

"I'm glad you're here."

Ross continued to hold her until someone's steps were heard in the hall. Mandy tried to get up when Mr. Brooks stuck his head in the door.

"No, no, stay where you are. I've just come to say good-bye and thank you for all you did."

"Thank me?" Mandy questioned him. "I didn't do anything, Mr. Brooks. I should be thanking you."

"Well, let's just say I admire your courage, Mandy, and I'm glad we're neighbors once again."

He was gone with those words, and Ross smiled at her surprised look. "He told me he hoped his own daughters would grow to be half as lovely and sweet as you and Carrie are."

"Oh!" Mandy was speechless.

"Now," Ross said firmly, "are you up to hearing a little story?"

"Sure, I guess so." She eyed Ross almost warily as he moved to the middle of the room and caught her eyes with his own.

"My story is about a boy who had a woman come into his life, a woman who was a few years older than he was. Well, this boy was sure he was in love with that woman. But she wasn't the one for him. Instead she introduced him to the greatest love of all—Jesus Christ. The boy was hungry to be loved by God and know Him personally, and he reached out and was saved by grace.

"Then a miraculous thing happened—the boy had a chance to lead a girl to the Lord, a girl he'd cared about for a long time. The boy thought his life was complete. He knew Christ and this special girl knew Christ. It seemed a perfect match.

"But it wasn't what God intended for the boy, and as the boy grew into manhood God asked him to move away from home and practice law in Baxter.

"He obeyed God and moved, believing as he did that he'd seen it all. But then he looked into the hazel eyes of a small brunette and realized he hadn't seen anything.

"The man found those eyes haunting him—he saw them day and night. The man leaned on God for strength, and God was his support. Then, miracle of miracles, the woman with the hazel eyes came to know Christ. But life was still not complete.

"So afraid of making a mistake, this man held back and hurt the woman he loved. The woman he *now* knows he's supposed to marry."

Mandy's eyes had grown quite round, and she pushed herself back against the headboard. She watched Ross draw a gold chain from his breast pocket as he came to sit beside her on the bed.

"Amanda, will you please take this man? This man who loves you from the very depths of his soul?"

Mandy didn't look at the chain, or the lovely heart and pearl. Her eyes were locked with those of the most precious man on earth. Her hands came up and gently cradled his face. With loving fingertips she traced his cheeks and spoke in a whisper.

"Yes, Ross, I'll take this man."

They leaned toward each other and shared a soft kiss. Mandy's eyes were wet, and she could feel Ross' heart pound.

"You're supposed to notice the necklace," he teased, his voice not quite steady.

"It's beautiful," she answered still looking at him. "Just beautiful."

Epilogue

"Dad!" seven-and-a-half-year-old Becca called to Silas as she approached.

"What is it? Becca?"

"Eliza says I'm not an aunt. I am too an aunt, aren't I, Dad?"

"Yes, honey, you are. Mandy's baby is your niece."

"I told her so," Becca said with satisfaction. Mark, who was listening nearby, followed to have a talk with his daughter. Silas went back to his conversation with his sister-in-law, Abby.

"Amy and I have talked about visiting Bayfield, and I know we will. Has the church really doubled?"

"Yes, it has. Some weeks Paul cries tears of joy as he looks out over those full pews. I—" tears flooded Abby's eyes and Silas touched her shoulder in understanding. Paul and Abby's twin girls ran by then, followed closely by their brother Timothy.

"I'm in the same condition, Abby," Silas spoke again. "Levi and Clovis spent most of the summer with Amy's dad in Neillsville. They both came back having made decisions for Christ. Becca made a decision last year. Now all five of my—" his voice broke.

"Amy told me." Abby was barely able to get the words out.

Paul came over then and took the baby from her arms. He easily guessed what they were discussing when he saw his wife's and brother's tears.

"I hate to interrupt, Red, but it's our turn with the photographer."

"Oh, Paul! The girls just ran by and Timmy was chasing them. He's a mess."

248

"I'll get him and keep Matt. You get the girls. *And* you look beautiful," he added, when her hands moved anxiously to her hair.

— ✣ —

"Hiding out?"

"Oh, Preston," Emily laughed up at her husband of almost two years as he entered the kitchen. He kissed her and asked what she was writing.

"I want to be sure I write down everyone who's here. I think I've got them all."

"Let's see the list." He took the paper and read out loud.

> Preston and Emily Culver
>
> Luke and Christine Cameron—
> Joshua, Kathrine, Rachael, and Grace
>
> Mark and Susanne Cameron—
> Emily, Elizabeth, Ellen, Erika, and Esther
>
> Silas and Amy Cameron—
> Carrie, Levi, Clovis, and Rebecca
>
> John and Julia MacDonald—
> Calvin, Charles, and Robyn
>
> Paul and Abigail Cameron—
> Jessica, Julie, Timothy, and Matthew
>
> Ross and Amanda Beckett—
> Kimberly
>
> Peter Culver
>
> Grant Nolan
>
> Chad and April Nolan
>
> Maggie Pearson

"Looks complete to me. I heard Julia say that supper is served as soon as the group picture is taken.

"We had better make ourselves available."

Pete and Carrie came in just as Preston opened the door. "We're rounding everyone up for the picture."

"We were on our way."

"Okay," Pete said with a smile, and the older couple watched them go off hand in hand.

"He's loved her since she was 14," Preston mentioned as they went outside.

"It's been the same for her," Grandma Em added. "She told me there wasn't anything she could do about it. She's loved Pete from the moment she laid eyes on him and she's never even looked at anyone else."

"We Culver men love for life." He put his arm around her as they walked, and many of the family watched them smile at each other, causing their own faces to crease with delight.

It had not been a complete surprise that Preston wanted to marry Grandma Em. None of her grandchildren would have denied her the joy of his companionship, and in truth, they found him delightful. What *did* surprise most everyone was to see that they married for *love* not companionship, something that was very evident whenever they were in the same room together.

— ❖ —

"Okay, folks," the small man behind the camera called to them. "You'll have to come in close—that's right. Everyone look this way."

He gave instructions, which the adults tried to follow. The children, hungry and never wanting to stand still, squirmed and tried the patience of the ones who wanted the photo to be perfect.

When the photographer was satisfied, supper was served on long tables outside. Food and good fellowship was plentiful. Everyone sang to Mark's Emily, whose birthday was only a few days away. Paul was elected to say a few words, and when he stood, even the children were quiet.

"I know I speak for Abby and myself when I say it's wonderful to be here. And thank you for giving me this chance to speak. Being the only one to live away from Baxter, well, let's just say we feel the miles very keenly at times. Please know that we love you, miss you, and pray for you.

"The words seem insignificant when I say them, but say them I will—God has been good, hasn't He? I love standing here and seeing our family together again, gathered not only as a family but gathered with our memories too. I love having my wife by my side with our four wonderful children.

"I love looking over at Silas holding his *granddaughter*." Paul's eyes twinkled and everyone laughed as the very young grandfather snuggled Mandy's little Kimberly close and kissed her.

Paul's eyes went to Ross and became moist. "We've come a long way, haven't we, Ross?" The younger man nodded, choked up as well, his arm around Mandy.

"It's good to have Grant here. I hear his summer with the boys was very blessed. And my congratulations go to my niece Carrie; I hope we can make it back for the wedding." Pete and Carrie smiled at him from their place and then at one another.

Paul looked for a long minute at his grandmother and Preston. He then spoke with emotion. "It's good to have you with us, Preston. There isn't any way to describe to you how precious it is to us that you love our grandmother as we do. And her beautiful countenance tells us she loves you in return. We thank God for you.

"I'll close now with these words out of Second Thessalonians, the last verses. 'Now the Lord of peace himself give you peace always by all means. The Lord be with you all. The salutation of Paul with mine own hand, which is the token in every epistle; so I write. The grace of our Lord Jesus Christ be with you all. Amen.'"

Books by Lori Wick

A Place Called Home Series
A Place Called Home
A Song for Silas
The Long Road Home
A Gathering of Memories

The Californians
Whatever Tomorrow Brings
As Time Goes By
Sean Donovan
Donovan's Daughter

Kensington Chronicles
The Hawk and the Jewel
Wings of the Morning
Who Brings Forth the Wind
The Knight and the Dove

Rocky Mountain Memories
Where the Wild Rose Blooms
Whispers of Moonlight
To Know Her by Name
Promise Me Tomorrow

The Yellow Rose Trilogy
Every Little Thing About You
A Texas Sky
City Girl

Contemporary Fiction
Sophie's Heart
Beyond the Picket Fence (Short Stories)
Pretense
The Princess
Bamboo & Lace
Bamboo & Lace Audio Book

Gift Books
Reflections of a Thankful Heart